KU-072-901

BOLTON
WITHDRAWN
FROM
STOCK
LIBRARIES

BT 1466942 0

Claire Messud is a recipient of Guggenheim and Radcliffe Fellowships and the Strauss Living Award from the American Academy of Arts and Letters. She lives in Cambridge, Massachusetts with her husband and children.

THE BURNING GIRL

Julia Robinson and Cassie Burnes have been friends since nursery school. They have shared everything, including their desire to escape the stifling limitations of their birthplace, the quiet town of Royston, Massachusetts. While Julia comes from a stable, happy middle-class family, Cassie never knew her father, who died when she was an infant, and has an increasingly tempestuous relationship with her mother, Bev. As the two girls enter adolescence, their paths diverge. When Bev becomes involved with the mysterious Anders Shute, Cassie feels cruelly abandoned. Disturbed, angry and desperate for answers, she sets out on a journey that will put her own life in danger, and shatter her oldest friendship.

CLAIRE MESSUD

THE BURNING GIRL

Complete and Unabridged

CHARNWOOD
Leicester

First published in Great Britain in 2017 by
Fleet
an imprint of Little, Brown Book Group
London

First Charnwood Edition
published 2018
by arrangement with
Little, Brown Book Group
London

*A catalogue record for this book is available
from the British Library.*

ISBN 978–1–4448–3680–6

Published by
F. A. Thorpe (Publishing)
Anstey, Leicestershire

Set by Words & Graphics Ltd.
Anstey, Leicestershire
Printed and bound in Great Britain by
T. J. International Ltd., Padstow, Cornwall

This book is printed on acid-free paper

For Livia, Lucian & James
And in memory of C.H.

Love's the boy stood on the burning
deck trying to recite 'The boy stood on
the burning deck.' Love's the son stood
stammering elocution while the poor
ship in flames went down.

. . . And love's the burning boy.

ELIZABETH BISHOP,
from 'Casabianca'

PART ONE

You'd think it wouldn't bother me now. The Burneses moved away long ago. Two years have passed. But still, I can't lie in the sun on the boulders at the quarry's edge, or dangle my toes in the cold, clear water, or hear the other girls singing, without being aware the whole time that Cassie is gone. And then I want to say something — but you can't, you know. It's like she never existed.

So either I don't go out there in the first place, or I end up coming straight home, dropping my bike on the back lawn with its wheels still spinning, and banging the screen door so loudly that my mother startles each time, and bustles through to the kitchen and looks at me, her eyes filled with emotions that I glimpse one after the other — love, fear, frustration, disappointment, but love, mostly. She usually says only one word — 'Thirsty?' — with a question mark, and that word is the bridge from there to here, and I either say 'Yep' or 'Nope' and she either pours me water from the jug in the fridge or she doesn't. We take it from there, we move on.

In this way the days pass and will keep passing — wasn't it Cassie herself who used to say, 'It's all just a question of time passing'? — and we'll get to the end of this summer, the way we got to the end of the last one, the way we got through all that happened over two years ago now. Each day puts a little more distance between now and then, so I can believe — I have to believe — that someday I'll look back and 'then' will be a speck on the horizon.

It's a different story depending on where you start: who's good, who's bad, what it all means. Each of us shapes our stories so they make sense of who we think we are. I can begin when Cassie and I were best friends; or I can begin when we weren't anymore; or I can begin at the dark end and tell it all backward.

There's no beginning 'before,' though: Cassie and I met at nursery school, and I can't remember a time when I didn't know her, when I didn't pick her sleek white head out of a crowd and know exactly where she was in a room, and think of her, some ways, as mine. Cassie was tiny, with bones like a bird. She was always the smallest girl in the class, and the span of her ankle was the span of my wrist. She had shiny, white-blond hair, almost albino she was so fair, her skin translucent and a little pink. But you'd be wrong to mistake her size and pallor for frailty. All you had to do was to look into her eyes — still blue eyes that turned gray in dark weather, like the water in the quarry — and you could see that she was tough. *Strong*, I guess, is a better word. Although of course in the end she wasn't strong enough. But even when we were small, she had a quality about her, a what-the-hell, an 'I'm not chicken, are *you*?' sort of way.

According to my mother, and to Cassie's

mother, Bev, Cassie and I became friends in the second week of nursery when we were four years old. That was always the story, though I can't tell now whether I remember it, or have just been told so many times that I invented the memory. I was playing with a group of kids in the sandbox, and Cassie stood in the middle of the playground, hands at her sides like a zombie, staring at everything, not apparently nervous, but totally detached. I left my friends to come touch her elbow, and I said — so I was told — 'Hey, come build a castle with me?' And she broke into that rare, broad smile of hers, a famous smile, made all the better when she was bigger by the Georgia Jagger gap between her front teeth. She came with me back to the sandbox. 'And that,' my mother always said, 'was that.'

When you're in nursery school, you don't think too much about it. Both only children, we said that the other was the sister we never had. Nobody could mistake us for blood relations — I was as tall for my age and as big-boned as Cassie was small, and my hair is dark and curly. But we shared our blue eyes. 'Look at our eyes,' we'd say, 'we're secret sisters.'

I knew her house and her bedroom as well as I knew my own. Cassie lived with her mother on a dead-end side road off Route 29 at the entrance to town, in a newish subdivision built in the '90s, when the economy was good. A perfect little Cape house on the outside, it looked as though it had been picked up from somewhere else and plopped on its modest plot of land: a white house with red shutters, dormer windows, a long, sloping dark roof, and a careful skirt of lawn out front, a little skimpy and each year more weedy, until it was more crabgrass and clover than lawn, and a funny white picket fence, just a *U* of fence, with a gate at the front walk, but it didn't go all the way around the house — an ornamental fence, I guess you'd call it. Just beyond the fence and behind the house spread nature unadulterated, rampant Queen Anne's lace and maple saplings, eager acacias and elders reaching for the sky, and beyond this first wildness, the dark northeastern forest, not twenty feet from the back of the house, a constant reminder that the trees and hawks and deer and bears — we saw a mother and her cubs on the tarmac of the cul-de-sac one time, on their way to check out the garbage cans — had been there long before humans showed up, and would surely be there long after.

The word that comes to mind is 'encroaching': it felt like the forest was encroaching on the Burneses' house, although in truth of course it was the other way around: the developers had made humans encroach upon nature. Houses stood on either side of the Burneses', bigger models than theirs, plain cedar shingles rather than white, surrounded by swollen hungry bushes. The family on one side, the Aucoins, kept two German shepherds, often outside, that terrified us when we were small. Cassie always claimed one of the Aucoins' houseguests had had a hole bitten out of his butt by the bitch, Lottie, but this couldn't have been right, I realize now, or the Aucoins would've had to have Lottie put down. Cassie liked a good story, and it wasn't so important that it be strictly true.

Cassie's mother, Bev, was a nurse, but not a regular nurse in a hospital. She worked in hospice care and every day she drove in her burgundy Civic full of files and equipment to the homes of the dying, to make sure they were comfortable, or as comfortable as they could be. My father, who isn't religious — who won't even go to church at Christmas with my mother and me — said that Bev did 'God's work.'

Bev was always cheerful — or almost always, except when she wasn't — and matter-of-fact about her job. Devoutly Christian, she didn't get teary about her clients dying — she always said 'passing' — and she spoke as though she was helping them to prepare for a mysterious but possibly amazing trip, rather than helping them to prepare for a hole in the ground.

Bev had big, soft breasts and a broad behind. She wore long, flowy printed skirts that swirled when she walked. Only her delicate hands and feet reminded me of Cassie. Bev's greatest vanity was her hands: her fingernails were always perfectly manicured, oval and filed and painted pretty colors like hard candies. That and her hair, a sweet-smelling honey-colored cloud. When you hugged Bev, you smelled her hair.

My mother was not at all like Bev, just as my house is not at all like Cassie's. And I have a father, and in that sense we were always different. For a long time, Cassie liked being at our house because she could pretend that we really *were* secret sisters, that my family was her family too.

My parents settled in Royston not long after my father finished school, before I was born. When they moved into our house it must have seemed as vast as a castle: a ramshackle hundred-and-fifty-year-old Victorian with five bedrooms, a wraparound porch, and a building behind that used to be stables. Not fancy, just old. The kitchen is older than my mother — a 1950s kitchen, with white cupboards that don't close all the way and black-and-white checker-board lino — and when the furnace kicks in, it sounds like a cruise ship.

My father is a dentist, and he has his office in the stables. On the big lawn, a shield-shaped shingle announces DR. RICHARD ROBINSON, DENTIST, DDS, FACS in black capitals. It squeaks when it's windy. When he goes to work, he walks a hundred feet out the back door. On the other hand, when someone has a toothache at ten o'clock at night, they know just where to find him. Tracy Mann, the hygienist, comes in on Mondays, Wednesdays, and Fridays, and dad's assistant, Anne Boudreaux, has been there every weekday since I can remember. She's about the same age as my parents but seems older, maybe because she wears a lot of makeup. She has a dark mole on her upper lip like Marilyn Monroe, but on Anne it isn't what you'd call sexy.

My mother is a freelance journalist, a vagueness that seems to mean she can be a journalist when it suits her. She writes restaurant and movie reviews for the *Essex County*

Gazette, and for the past few years she's written a literary blog that has a following, including an adult English class in Tokyo that writes very polite comments. The third floor of our house is her office — my friend Karen's dad did the renovation when I was in first grade. Karen moved to Minneapolis when we were nine.

My room is next to the bathroom on the middle floor, facing to the side, with a view toward the Saghafis' next door. They put in an aboveground pool a few summers ago, and I hear their kids splashing around all season long. As soon as it's warm enough to keep my window wide open, they're out there. The Saghafis said we should feel free to come over and use the pool anytime, but I don't anymore, because their kids are an awkward amount younger than I am, and always in the water.

I did, though, the first summer they had it. My father called the pool 'an eyesore,' but my mother said, 'let people have their fun.' She said I should take them up on their open invitation, that we'd seem standoffish if we didn't. I went almost every day with Cassie, that summer. I'd just turned twelve: the summer before seventh grade. The Saghafi kids, still too young to swim without their mom's supervision, weren't around nearly as much then, and Cassie and I spent entire afternoons swimming and tanning and talking, then swimming and tanning and talking some more, with great deliberation, as though we followed to the letter a complicated recipe.

If I could go back, I'd write it all down: the secrets we told each other and the plans we made. The songs we listened to, even, when we turned up her iPod so it sounded like a scratchy transistor radio: 'California Gurls' by Katy Perry, and that hit Rihanna made with Eminem, so catchy but creepy when you actually listened to the words. '*Stand there and watch me burn . . .*' My mother changed the station when it came on in the car, shaking her head and saying 'Girls, I'm sorry, but as a feminist, I object.'

It was the summer of my stars-and-stripes bikini — the top, stars; the bottom, stripes — and I was proud that when I lay flat on my back, the bottom stretched from hip bone to hip bone. In between there was a dip, my stomach was a dip, and if I lifted my head a little and looked down, I could glimpse the dark curling hair between my legs that was newly there. Cassie, so fair, had to wear a ton of sunblock, and even so, she'd burn wherever she missed a bit. I remember the night she slept over and the backs of her thighs, near her knees, were almost purple. My mother soaked cloths in vinegar and laid them on the burn to take away some of the heat. Cassie shrieked when the first cloth went on, but she didn't cry. Cassie almost never cried.

That same summer, we volunteered at the animal shelter out of town on Route 29, and each adopted a kitten. The kittens were sisters, from the same litter, two tortoiseshells, small enough then to hold in your hand, with tiny white teeth and opalescent claws that dug pulsingly but painlessly into your jeans when you set the creatures on your lap. She named hers Electra. I called mine Xena, after the warrior princess, because it sounded good alongside Electra. Xena is now a plump and placid puff of fur on the cusp of middle age, whose warrior nature extends only to chasing birds and mice under cover of darkness — she brings us occasional mangled offerings and deposits them on the kitchen floor, as if we might fry them up for breakfast — but within a year, Electra, still small, had vanished in the night.

She was an adventurer, and from early on went marauding in the forest behind Cassie's house. There came the time, not long after Anders Shute moved into the Burneses' lives, that Electra simply never came home. If she'd been hit by a car out on Route 29, we would've found her corpse. We wondered if she'd been kidnapped by a person or stolen by a hawk, or whether her tiny skeleton lay somewhere among the rotting leaves in the Encroaching Forest. Cassie liked to imagine that Electra had slipped off to join another family, maybe even a mile or two down the road, and that she was happily devouring tuna from a silver bowl: a better new life. 'If you have to imagine, why imagine something bad?' she'd say. I was the one who was sure she must be dead.

That summer, we both wanted to be veterinarians, among other things. I was going to be a vet, a pop star, and a writer — although, I'd sometimes reflect, being a writer of pop songs might be good enough; then I'd be just a vet and a pop star — and Cassie wanted to be a vet, an actress, and a fashion stylist. We flipped repeatedly through *Tiger Beat* — my mom had got me a subscription because of my interest in music, and because she'd had one when she was young. I was interested in what the bands sounded like; Cassie rated them on how they looked. Her mother had explained that there were people out in Hollywood or in New York who made a living choosing the outfits for celebrities to wear. Bev didn't say this like it was a good thing; more like, *We live in such a crazy world that some people think this is an acceptable way to spend your life!* But that's not how Cassie took it. She loved fashion. We'd dawdle in the makeup aisle at Rite Aid while she tested every different eye shadow on the back of her hand. I pretended to be into it because she loved it so much. She thought Lady Gaga was cool not for her songs but for her fashion sense: those crazy shoes; that dress made out of meat. And partly, maybe, because you couldn't get further from Bev Burnes than Lady Gaga.

Bev approved of our desire to become vets. She encouraged it. She was the one who approached my mother and suggested that if they split the driving, it wouldn't be a hassle for us to work at the shelter. My mother agreed it would introduce us to 'adult responsibility.' 'When I was young, in Philadelphia, I was a candy striper at the hospital,' she told us. The volunteers had the name because they wore red-and-white striped pinafores. 'I pushed people around the hospital in wheelchairs,' she recalled, 'from their rooms to X-ray, or from the ER to their rooms. To Physical Therapy. To the hairdresser even, sometimes. One old lady would clap her hands when she saw me, and cry, 'My girl! My girl!'' She told us about turning a corner too hard and ramming a woman's outstretched broken leg, encased in plaster, into a wall. Even many years later she couldn't stifle an embarrassed laugh: 'From how loudly she yelped, it must have hurt a lot.' I guess it seemed to her safer for us to hang out with animals, but still in the spirit of 'service.' Bev and my mother were both big on the idea of 'service,' of 'giving back,' expressions that were meant to remind us of how fortunate we were.

Royston isn't a wealthy town, in spite of the Henkel plant not far away; and in spite of the fact that the nearby towns, like Newburyport and Ipswich, are on the water and attract wealthy people, especially in the summer. If, in the terms of, say, Boston, the Robinsons are negligible, in Royston we're pretty privileged. Even Bev and Cassie were privileged, in their modest way.

The animal shelter, a one-story breeze-block building, felt like a cross between the vet's and a kennel. The air-conditioned front room had navy plastic chairs set up on the linoleum tile, like a waiting room, and a high counter behind which sat one or two real employees with computers and files. It smelled like Band-Aids and was always cold, like a walk-in freezer. On the dun-colored walls hung posters about caring for animals and vaccinations ('Heartworm: the heartbreaking killer'; 'Lyme Disease and Your Pet'), and along one side of the room stretched a big bulletin board plastered with photographs of dogs and cats alongside their new owners.

Marj, the woman in charge — small, wiry, and brown — had short graying hair that looked as though she cut it herself, and a scratchy voice. Her loose tank tops bared her muscly arms. Underneath, her old-lady boobs dangled flat and wide somewhere just above her navel. Cassie and I had pictured our veterinary selves in professional white coats and smart, clicky low-heeled pumps, and while Marj wasn't a vet (when a vet was needed, Dr. Murphy came in from Haverhill, bluff and bearded, his belly tight beneath his white coat), she gave us a different sense of how you could be in the world: someone who did what you did for the love of it, and didn't care what anybody thought.

Marj really loved those animals. Her leather hands were all pop-up veins, but when she touched the tottering, one-eyed pug Stinky on his rippled tummy, she was tender, and when she held a skittish cat like Loulou to her loose bosom, the cat's wild eyes would quickly grow heavy, her body slack, and she'd emit the low, motorized hum of feline pleasure. Marj was especially good with the pit bulls and pit crosses that the shelter got in such numbers. Most people were afraid of them, even just a little, and Cassie and I were considered too young to take on their care; but Marj approached each one as if he were a long-lost friend, murmuring in a low voice, careful but sure. They called her the Pit Whisperer, but it didn't always work out well. She had the scars to prove it.

You entered the animal shelter through a heavy metal door next to the admin counter. The cattery came first, still air-conditioned but less chilly, a big room with floor-to-ceiling cages about four feet by four feet, in which cats of all shapes, sizes, and colors dozed or groomed or paced in the palpable ammonia fug of kitty litter and sweet antiseptic. Sometimes a rabbit hovered, twitching, down at the far end, and once, a ferret named Fred, skittering around his cage as if late for an appointment.

Even there, you heard the dogs through the wall — they never stopped barking, an endless echoing disharmony. At the shelter, dogs were the important thing. Moving out to their kennel, you passed into a world of sound and heat and motion. The sticky summer air smacked at you, the sudden volume frantic. But in summer the kennels had their sides up, so the breeze blew right through. With the flick of a latch, each dog could slip out to the chicken wire runs that spanned the length of the building. The dogs were kept two or three to a cage: many runaway or abandoned animals got picked up or dropped off because their owners couldn't manage them any longer. The little old dogs came in because their little old owners had died, or got sick, or gone to live in apartments that wouldn't accept pets. It was hard to find homes for them — Stinky was one; and Elsie, a ten-year-old shih tzu with an incontinence problem; or Fritzl, the swaybacked deaf dachshund that barked almost constantly. These little dogs lived closest to the metal door; then the middle range of large, loping youngsters, mixed breeds with beautiful dog faces, dogs that wanted to roam; and finally, farthest from the entrance, the pits and their kin, with their powerful jaws and sleek, close fur, one or two so snarly that they were kept muzzled.

Cassie and I went to the shelter two mornings a week, from nine till one. Our job was to feed the animals and clean out their cages. We wore rubber boots and rubber gloves and we got used to the smells; and it felt like a triumph when a scared, shy dog got used to you, and instead of cowering, inched toward you and dipped her head or rolled onto her back for a rub. The dogs were mostly sweet at heart. They wanted to be loved, and when you loved them, they loved you back.

We had our favorites — mine, a trim, glossy chocolate Lab mix called Delsey, with a chiseled, square face and dark, sad eyes, was only just past puppyhood, and moved his body as if its size was still a surprise to him. Although his eyes were mournful, his temperament was happy; he loved nothing more than playing fetch in the dog run with an old tennis ball or a stick. He'd bring the slobbery catch, and you could see him debating whether to let it go or not, weighing the choice between keeping his prize or getting to run after it again. Sometimes he'd lope off still carrying it, head up, tail up, like an athlete running a victory lap around the dog run.

Cassie's favorite, Sheba, was a pit cross. We were allowed to feed her but we weren't supposed to go into her cage unless Marj was there too; not because of Sheba herself, whose brindle face was almost smiley and who wagged her stumpy tail at the sight of us, but because her stall mate was a grumpy black bull named Leo, who didn't chase sticks but chewed them into splinters given the chance.

Cassie liked Sheba because she was beautiful but tough, a survivor. The story was she'd been found scrawny and starving in an outdoor pen next to an abandoned double-wide about ten miles inland in the backwoods. Her owners had skipped out — Cassie and I made up different stories about what had happened to them — and a couple of hunters heard the howling. They called Animal Control to come and rescue her. Cassie had asked her mother if they could adopt Sheba, but Bev had said categorically no, that any dog was too much for the two of them to manage, but that especially a dog like Sheba would be wrong, because after all she'd been through, Sheba needed a family that could spend a lot of time with her, spoil her, and make her feel loved.

Cassie liked to pretend that Sheba was her dog. There didn't seem to be any harm in it. Early on, when Leo was out of their cage one morning, Cassie slipped the latch and walked right in. Sheba, ecstatic, twitched and whimpered, and when Cassie sat down cross-legged on the concrete floor, Sheba ran over to be petted. She widened her eyes and flipped over, baring her spotted belly with its tiny unused teats, and Cassie rubbed her furiously, both of them emitting jumbled, excited little moans of pleasure.

I lurked in the hallway with my eye on the metal door: if she got caught, wouldn't we get sent home in disgrace?

But when I called to her, quietly — 'Hurry up, Cassie . . . come out . . . I think I hear someone!' — she first paid no attention and then got annoyed.

'What's your problem, Juju? Aren't we here to make their lives better? She loves it — don't you, my Sheba? Don't you, my darling?'

She didn't get caught — we didn't get caught — and by the time Nancy and Jo from the front office came in with some prospective adopters, we were back down the other end, Cassie sluicing out Stinky's cage with water while I held his raspy little pug body in my arms. But Cassie had staked her claim. After that, she was always looking for a chance to get into Sheba's cage, as if Sheba were her bad-boy boyfriend.

On a Thursday in early August when we'd been working at the shelter for almost two months, and we felt, and they felt, that we were as familiar as the furniture, Leo was in the run outside, getting some air, if the muggy swamp of that day could be called 'air.' He was alone — no other dogs, no human keeping an eye — and Marj had gone to take a phone call from the pet-food supplier about a delivery mix-up the previous day.

'You girls keep at it,' she'd said, 'I'll be right back.'

Once the door clanged behind Marj, Cassie hustled up to sneak a visit with Sheba. She had in her pocket a rawhide chew brought from home — bought with her own money, in fact. Rawhide chews weren't allowed at the kennel, not least because they could get stuck in a dog's throat and choke him; but Cassie didn't much care. She'd already slipped Sheba a couple, and knew she liked them so much she could gnaw one down in under three minutes flat. Just like the other times, Cassie slipped the latch and ducked into the cage, holding the treat high in her hand, to play a game with it. Even this she'd done before. While Sheba was playful, she wasn't aggressive by nature; so we didn't even think.

I didn't see all that happened next. My eyes were on the metal door, anticipating Marj. I wasn't thinking about Cassie and Sheba.

I certainly wasn't thinking about Leo. Because the gate from their enclosure to the outdoors looked closed, it didn't occur to either of us to check the latch. What were the odds that Leo would tire, just then, of his solo ramble in the dog run, that he would nose his way back home and push the gate open with his snout? But he did, somehow in the brief moment when Cassie held the rawhide in her hand.

He leaped for the chew, jaws gaping, paws uplifted. He clamped down on Cassie's left hand, gored her inner forearm. Thank God she had the chew to give over. Thank God. She barely squealed — Leo's snarling and Sheba's high, desperate barks made me whip around and look, not any noise from Cassie herself — and if I hadn't dragged her out of the cage ass-backward and kicked the door shut behind us, I don't know what might have happened.

It looked like she'd stuck her forearm in a wood-chipper, her skin shredded in strips up from the wrist, the blood coming so fast it dripped onto the floor.

'Can you wiggle your fingers?' I asked. That was what my mother asked me when I hurt myself. 'Can you move your wrist? How bad is it? Does it hurt?'

'I don't fucking know.' She slumped against the wire of the opposite cage, behind which an arthritic, white-muzzled pit named Opie stared with intent curiosity. 'I don't even know how it hurts.'

'Fuck, fuck, fuck.' I didn't know what else to say. My mother always says that cursing indicates an inadequate vocabulary and a poor imagination; but in this case, it seemed like just the right word. I leaned in close to Cassie's mangled hand, as if I might just touch it, but it was a pulsating bloody thing, and I couldn't. I was only vaguely aware of Leo and Sheba growling at each other in their barely closed cage right next to us, but Cassie was. She closed her eyes and started to shake.

'It's all fine. It's going to be fine. I'd better get Marj.' I got to my feet and double-checked the bolt on the grille. I floated in a strange quiet, watching, as though this was happening to other people. Then, in the hush inside my head, suddenly I heard the cacophony of the dogs up and down the hallway. They all barked at once, wild decibels, and I marveled that we'd been held, those few moments, in a terrible bubble of silence.

Walking to the metal door, I had my back to Cassie, I'd actually turned away from her, but it felt like she was a part of me. In the bedlam of the barking, stinking dogs and the hot, wet breeze gusting in from outside with its faint smell of hay, she and I were joined by an invisible thread, and that thread was no less real than everything else, and because of that thread she would be fine, Cassie would be fine, and she wouldn't even really be alone when I went through the door into the main building, because we were umbilically linked and inseparable.

Marj came through the door before I ever reached it. She saw in an instant what had happened, or enough of it anyway. Even as she ran down to Cassie, she paged Jo to bring the first-aid kit, and she wrapped a blanket around Cassie's shoulders because of the shock, and had her raise her arm up to stop the bleeding, and when she ascertained the sequence of events, more or less, the only words she had for me were 'Why'd you leave her?' As if somehow the whole thing, from beginning to end, were the fault of my inattention.

After she'd got her cleaned up, Marj decided that Cassie needed to go over to the hospital in Haverhill and get it checked out. Marj tried Bev, but the phone went straight to voicemail, so she called my mother and explained the situation and she agreed we'd take Cassie. It was logical. Nobody said anything at that point about whether we'd be allowed back in the shelter — after all, we'd broken the most important rules, and even though we didn't admit it, Marj must've known it wasn't the first time — but we did feel the pall of adult disapproval, that sense that you're being helped and punished at the same time.

By the time we came back to the shelter, Leo had been put down. He was dead. As a dog, and especially as an unloved dog, you couldn't attack a child and get away with it. But of course we knew, and Marj without saying it aloud made sure that we knew, that Leo hadn't done anything wrong: we'd entered his space, with a tantalizing rawhide chew, and he had merely acted as millennia of genetic imprinting dictated such a dog would act, within the parameters of a rather vicious and impatient canine nature. We must never forget that Cassie's act — and mine too, I guess, because I was her accomplice, like the bank robber who drives the getaway car — had brought about Leo's death as surely as if we'd wrung his neck with our bare hands.

But that was later. In the first instance, my mother showed up in the station wagon to take us to the ER. Grim-faced, she played NPR loudly on the radio the whole way so that there could be no conversation. We made the drive to Haverhill listening to a phone-in about the migration patterns of owls, until one caller talked about having hit a giant owl with his car as he crested a hill on a back road at dusk. That was too much for the day, so my mother turned the radio off altogether. Then we listened to the air conditioner blow. I sat on my hands, a reflexive position of childhood guilt, and something Cassie obviously couldn't do just then.

At the hospital, the nurse who untied Cassie's bandage crinkled her features at what she saw. Cassie had such delicate limbs, and even after all our tanning, her skin was so fair. Swollen, her hand was purpled and blackened with clotting blood, with deep scratches, tears almost, up her arm. The fingers didn't quite sit straight. She couldn't wiggle them, or barely. The nurse cleaned it carefully — even though Marj had already done that, it had bled some more — and Cassie yelped at the sting of the antiseptic. Just little yelps, though. Mostly she was quiet, watching her arm with her blue eyes wide, almost as if it was separate from her.

That was the first time we met Anders, or Dr. Shute, as he was to us then. Anders Shute was the doctor on call in the ER that afternoon. I made fun of him in the car on the way home, to try to make Cassie laugh — 'Do you think they bring the shooting victims to Dr. Shute?' and 'He looks like he's already been shot. Or maybe like he already shot someone himself. Doctor, don't shoot! Oh, shoot, it's Dr. Shute!'

He was tall and very thin, with pale, pale skin and protruding cheekbones like a death's head. His lips were thin, his nose was thin, his long fingers were thin, and his eyes had a squinty quality that made them look thin too. He had long hair like a girl's, down to his chin, and it too was thin, the kind of dishwater brown that looks greasy even when it's clean. Dr. Shute didn't have much of a bedside manner in the ER, but he wasn't horrible or anything, and when he took Cassie's mangled hand in his to look closely at it, I could tell that his gentleness surprised her: Cassie looked at him with some combination of beseeching and wonder, and for the first time she asked, 'Is my hand going to be okay?'

His smile was slight and — inevitably — thin, but he did make a special effort to warm his chilly eyes. 'Your hand, young lady, is going to be just fine. As long as you're a good patient, not an impatient patient — the '*im*-patient,' as we say around here — then your hand is going to be just fine.'

It struck me afterward that his was a slightly strange way of putting it, as if he were saying it was all up to her. If she would simply do the right thing, then her hand would heal. Which of course implied the fact (undeniable as it was) that if she hadn't done the *wrong* thing to begin with, she wouldn't be there at all. That's how he was, Anders Shute: the whole way along, from that first encounter, he made out like the ball was in Cassie's court: if she did the right thing, all would be well. And if she didn't — well, then.

He injected Cassie's hand with local anesthetic, and stapled the fine, frayed edges of her skin; he dressed the gouges up her arm with special unguents and pristine bandages, and he prescribed a course of horse-pill antibiotics to stave off any infection. No more nor less than any doctor would have done.

* * *

Bev bustled into our TV room later that afternoon with her stethoscope still around her neck, breathing heavily, a vision in blue florals, clearly torn between distress and anger. Although she enveloped Cassie in her arms first thing, I could see, which Cassie could not, that as she squeezed her daughter her expression was troubled, like a sky across which clouds are blowing at speed.

'My baby, my baby,' she murmured, 'what were you thinking? What were you thinking?' And then, 'Everything's all right. There we are, everything's all right now.'

My mother stood in the doorway watching them, drying her hands with a dish towel, and her expression struck me too: it wasn't forgiving. As if she'd drawn a circle around Bev and Cassie in her mind, and while they stood in the middle of our house, it didn't mean they belonged there. A look that seemed to say, *You aren't like us. Not entirely*.

There was no more swimming at the Saghafis', after that, because Cassie couldn't get her arm wet. And for a couple of weeks, we weren't sure if we'd be allowed back to the shelter. We had long empty days to fill, once Bev dropped Cassie off at my house before nine a.m. My mother wanted us out of her hair so she could work. She came up with a few chores — weeding the garden, sorting the books on the shelves in the TV room alphabetically by author — but she wasn't really serious about it, and nor were we, not least because Cassie's right hand — her writing hand — was out of commission. We couldn't even ride our bikes. We couldn't play tennis or basketball over at the high school, because for those things too you needed both hands.

'Really goes to show you,' Cassie said, flicking

her white-blond hair with the starchy white mitt of her dressed hand, 'how hard it is to have only one arm.'

'Do we know many people with only one arm?'

'Wendy's uncle,' she said, referring to a girl in our class. 'Lost it in Iraq. You've seen him. He works at the Lowe's in Haverhill.'

'Then there's Benny's grandpa.' Benny was a few years older. 'He had polio when he was young. He's got his hand, but it's all shriveled up and he can't do anything with it. He holds it like this.' I mimed the way Benny's grandpa held his arm against his middle, with the hand hanging down like an empty glove.

'Jesus,' Cassie said. 'That won't be me, will it?'

'Don't be silly. You heard the doctor. As long as you're a good patient . . . '

'But I'm the *im*-patient. I'm so *bored*. And this is going to go on for *weeks*.'

'Not weeks.'

'Whatever. Way too long. I don't want to bake any more chocolate-chip cookies. These are our *lives*, here. Before you know it, we'll be back at school, sitting in those horrible classrooms waiting for time to pass all over again. We've got to think up something to do.'

* * *

So we went out. My house is in town, or rather, on the way into town, at the south end. Town itself is about four long blocks in one direction, and five in the other, and then there are the two strip malls on Route 29 out to the highway, where Market Basket is, and the Dollar Store and the Fashion Bug, and Friendly's. There are more than four square blocks to Royston, but the rest of it is winding residential streets, petering out in all directions to forest, except Route 29 in both ways, with its smattering of businesses uninterrupted southward and again right up northward to Newburyport. It's quicker to get places on the interstate, but that way you miss the old stuff, like the Golden Lotus Palace restaurant, a vermilion temple to 1960s kitsch with a huge gilded gate and black plaster dragons outside, where the food is so spiked with MSG that you come out feeling like you're on another planet. Or the Lucky Stars motel, which finally went belly-up a few years ago: a couple of panels have fallen off the old neon sign — it looked like something out of *The Jetsons* when it was whole — and they boarded up the windows to keep homeless people and animals from squatting in the shag-rug rooms. There are these echoes of old Royston along Route 29, how it was before the Boston bourgeois exiles and the artists, and even before the Henkel plant.

Cassie and I went exploring on foot, which meant downtown, mostly. Until we made our way to the quarry and the old asylum. Downtown has a row of great old buildings, redbrick Victorian style, with apartments above the shops. I always wondered who lives in them. Many of the shopfronts don't last long — Royston is the kind of small town that people escape to from Boston or Portland, bringing their small children and their fantasies, only to find that village life isn't as simple as they'd expected. They set up a sparkly jewelry shop or a cute café with cows painted on the walls and frilly curtains, and stick it out through a year or even two, through bitter, lean winters when nobody's on the street; but sooner or later they shut up shop and head back where they came from. There are the long-timers too, the Adamian Pharmacy, and Mahoney's Irish Pub, and Bell's Dry Goods, run by crabby Mildred Bell, older than my grandmother and with a wart on her chin like a witch. Bell's, a crazy, cluttered place, sells, among other things, Christmas sweaters embroidered with reindeers or elves. They protect their never-changing display windows with yellow-tinted cellophane. When I was little, I liked it for the toy section, which includes a line of plastic bins containing stuff I could afford with my pocket money — Japanese erasers and Hello Kitty notepads, glow-in-the-dark Super Balls and hair clips in the shape of plaster hamburgers or cupcakes. Mrs. Bell must have a weakness for stuffed animals too, because they have a big wicker bin filled with the softest ones, not just bears but owls and giraffes and a great selection of pigs in particular. Cassie and I liked to go into Bell's that August to visit the stuffed animals, and because I felt bad about her hand and her hard time, I sneaked back on my own and bought her the littlest pig, palest pink, that she'd already named Hubert. I hid him for a surprise, but only for a day because when we were back in the shop and she saw he was missing, she wailed.

After Mrs. Bell's shop, and the Rite Aid where we liked best the aisle of trial-sized items and the nail polishes (although Cassie wasn't allowed to wear nail polish and I didn't want to), there weren't that many places in Royston for kids to go. We ambled over to the kiddie playground out Market Street past the high school, with the rainbow roundabout and the bank of swings, but that summer they were rebuilding the slide and the climbing structure, leaving only stumps, and besides, the other kids in the park were little, under five, accompanied by mothers or grandmas, and it was somehow more depressing than staying home.

Seeing as we couldn't play tennis or basketball, the high school wasn't fun; and besides, a loudmouthed eighth grader named Beckett hung out there with his friends, including the boy I had a crush on, Peter Oundle. He'd been at our school always, and when we were smaller we'd all played together at recess — tag, and four square, and touch football. Now, though, he hung out with Beckett, two years ahead of us and the leader of a gang, long-limbed, quick-footed boys with sneering mouths. Peter Oundle, only a year ahead of Cassie and me, had always felt different, the kind of boy who'd offer his hand to help you up when you fell. Skinny, pointy-nosed, but handsome: reddish-brown curls, long lashes.

The boys played pickup basketball games for hours. One or two of them wolf-whistled when we passed, and one afternoon Beckett called out to me, 'Hey, Curly, what are those huge pimples on your front?' which made the other boys guffaw and me flush with shame. Cassie shouted back, 'Envious, are you, Beckett? 'Cause I see you got your hair long, like a girl.'

'Aw, fuck you too,' Beckett shouted, and turned his back; but like he was embarrassed, I thought.

'I'd hug you right here,' I said to Cassie, 'but that would just prove to him that we're gay.'

'Who cares?' Cassie said. 'I'd marry you over him any day.'

We'd walked on and were passing the playground when Peter Oundle caught up to us. His curls were slick with sweat, his bony chest heaving under his mesh tank (Celtics, number 9). He touched me on the shoulder, and it burned. I was sure my face was red.

'Hey.' He stood a second.

'What do you want?' Cassie sounded disgusted.

'I just wanted to apologize.'

'What?' she said again.

'Beckett can seem like an asshole sometimes.'

'No kidding.'

'But he's not so bad. It was a joke.'

'Not funny.' Cassie glared at Peter like he'd said it himself.

'It's okay.' I smiled. 'I'll survive. Thanks for coming over.'

Peter nodded, and turned to run back to the game; but he looked back over his shoulder as he went, and smiled outright. At me, I thought, then: he came over for me.

'Shame he's turned into one of them,' Cassie said as we set off again.

'He's not so bad.'

She snorted, as if to say, *You wish*. She knew I liked him.

The quarry was where the older kids partied in the summer, and where we went swimming occasionally with our parents and their friends who belonged. It was about a mile west of Royston off a little county road, down a dirt track between two private houses. Abandoned over a hundred years ago, the old quarry is filled with glorious rare gray-green water, a color out of an old oil painting. In some lights, the great boulders gleam gold, but the word that comes to mind is 'tawny,' like a lion. The quarry itself is lion-colored, which is why the Royston Town Hall — built in the 1870s with its stones — is lion-colored also.

Strictly speaking, the quarry is a private pool. It belongs to the local Land Association, a group of trustees who bought up a bunch of acreage between Cape Ann and the New Hampshire border, and run it as a kind of nature charity. You're supposed to have a membership. Halfway along the dirt road, a chain hangs across it; but there's no lock on the chain, and if you're biking or walking you can slip around it. There's no lifeguard or caretaker, except Rudy, who also takes care of the cemetery: he drives over every so often unannounced in his dark orange pickup with his one-eyed German shepherd, Bessie, to make sure nothing crazy is going on. He's not a bad guy, Rudy, though he looks a little scary. He doesn't have all his teeth and his cheeks cave in on themselves as if his mouth were a pull-string. And Bessie — well, people are scared of German shepherds, and she's a surprising sight because one eye is milky and reflects the light.

That first afternoon, we saw him on the main road, headed into town as we headed out. We were on the gravel verge, and he made a showy loop to the other side of the road as he passed us, and raised his hand in an old-fashioned country wave and nodded our way. A toothpick, or an unlit cigarette, stuck up out of his mouth, and his greasy cap was on backward, wings of hair poking out below. Bessie had her head half out the window on the passenger side, tongue lolling, eating the breeze. The sight made us laugh: 'Dog joy,' Cassie said. 'Wish we could get us some.'

We wanted to walk out to the quarry simply to fill the time. We couldn't swim, or Cassie couldn't, on account of her hand; but it seemed the place to explore, not least because we knew one of the trails through the woods from the quarry led to the old asylum. Cassie thought that was the coolest thing: if we could find our way to the asylum, who knew what we'd discover? She had some idea there'd be treasure — something hidden or left behind, something we couldn't imagine until it was revealed.

'Maybe someone's even living there,' she suggested, raising her eyebrows and smiling. 'Somebody everybody thinks is gone.'

'That seems like a reason *not* to go looking.'

'Wimp.'

'I'm not. Besides, if anybody was living there, we'd know about it.'

'How?'

'That close to town? You don't just get away with stuff like that.'

'So, we could pretend to live there. Like, for the afternoon.'

We didn't play pretend games anymore because we were too grown-up, but secretly we missed them. A stage as big as an asylum seemed perfect: we could disappear into the woods to a secret hidey hole, and suddenly it would be okay to behave as though we were ten again, and she was a World War II Resistance fighter and I'd parachuted in from England on a secret mission; or we were the only two survivors after the apocalypse and had to live off nuts and berries and rainwater.

The woods around Royston are great for those kinds of games. There are clearings in the trees, and huge slabs of rock like tables, fallen logs to serve as benches, rocky overhangs underneath which you can build a little camp that will stay dry in all but the heaviest rainfall. They're not impenetrable, not a Hansel and Gretel forest, but a forest where the sunlight falls green and dappled to the soft, piney ground, where surprising toadstools sprout in clumps — flat red plates or piled cream ruffles, tiny yellow shiny bulbs, almost slick — and invisible birds call to one another in the high branches overhead. Sometimes you catch the bright flash of a red-winged blackbird or a cardinal, and upon occasion, at the quarry itself, a misguided preening egret teetering on its precarious pins, stretching its great wings and arching its prehistoric neck to glare at you from a bald, glittering eye.

On that first day we tramped out to the quarry, we saw such an egret. We called her Nancy, because the name made us laugh, and whenever we saw another after that, wherever it was, we waved and shouted, 'Hey, Nancy, good to see you!' We felt like she was a good omen, a sign for us.

Cassie took off her sneakers and socks and dangled her feet in the water, while I fussed about whether she'd get her dressed hand wet in a puddle at the water's edge, until she told me to shut up. It had been a hot walk, even under the trees, and I was tempted to strip off and plunge in, even for a minute, to make the swelling in my fingers and ankles go down. (Some people swell in the heat, and some people don't. Needless to say, Cassie didn't.) But I'd made myself the promise that I wouldn't, so I too sat on the hot stone and dabbled my puffy feet, listening to the cicadas scream and wishing for more. It had taken almost an hour to get there from my house, and it would take as long to get back, and we hadn't brought so much as a bottle of water.

As Nancy spread her wings and tucked her legs, lifting off like an airplane with barely a splash, Cassie threw back her head and narrowed her eyes. 'It's good here,' she said.

'Even better when we can swim.'

'It's so deep, isn't it?'

The water, in its gray-green-ness, was

intensely clear; and yet you couldn't see the bottom. 'What do you think is down there?'

'Stone, of course. It's a quarry.'

'Ghosts, though? Do you think there are ghosts?' We both knew the story of the teenager who'd drowned there, long before we were born. Back in the 1980s. A bunch of kids had come skinny-dipping at night, drunk or high or both, and this boy had dived in headfirst and hit his head on a rock and never come up again. The kids were so rowdy that they didn't even notice he wasn't with them until it was time to go home. And the police couldn't find his body until the next day. In Royston, we all knew that story from very young, although we knew it like a myth, not like a fact. We didn't know his name or anything. It was why there was a big sign at the parking lot that said no diving.

'Ghosts?' Cassie squinted at me in the bright sun. 'Don't tell me you believe in ghosts.'

'Don't tell me you don't.'

'Of course I don't.'

'What about your dad, then?'

Cassie shook her head and was quiet for a minute. 'That's not ghosts. That's angels. It's totally different. And it's not some stupid joke.' She pulled her feet out of the water and turned her back to me, crossing her legs and hanging her head like a turtle tucking in on itself.

'I wasn't — I didn't mean . . . Cass . . . I'm sorry, okay?'

She didn't turn around straightaway. When she did, she had a funny set to her mouth. I thought she was angry with me, and only afterward did it occur to me that she was trying not to cry. 'It's time to head back, don't you think?' she said. 'Didn't your mom promise grilled cheese?'

'And milkshakes. Chocolate.'

* * *

Cassie's father was as much a myth as the drowned boy. Not in the sense that he might not be real, but in the sense that she'd never actually known him. Or rather, that she couldn't remember him. Except his face: she said she had a memory of him leaning over her crib, his blue eyes, and of feeling safe held in the crook of his arm — infant memories, dark around the edges like an old photograph, but indelible. He had chosen her name, Cassandra, because he thought it was the most beautiful. And her bird bones came from his side, and her aptitude for math, or so Bev had told her. Her love of onion rings. Her stick-out ears.

My father is so present in my life that I don't really even look at him. Not properly. I love him, fiercely, but in some way I barely see him. He makes bad puns and my mother and I groan. He gets angry about my gear cluttering up the front hall, and I roll my eyes. I know his face so well that I can't tell when it's changing — my mother pointed out the other day that more than half his hair is gray now: when did that happen? How could I not have noticed? He said that's what family is for: the people who love you see you in the best light, as you want to be seen. He made out it wasn't just because I hadn't been looking.

Whereas for Cassie, it was as if her father stood behind a thick black curtain with a few tiny holes in it. She had to get up close to those pinpricks and peer through, trying to glean her father's overall shape from the little she could glimpse.

Bev had told her the story a thousand times, about how he died. They were living in a farmhouse about forty minutes northwest of Boston when Cassie was born, and Bev, though she'd finished her coursework, hadn't yet qualified as a nurse. Cassie's father, whose name was Clarke — 'Clarke Burnes, that's a good name, right?' Cassie whispered, whenever we talked about it, like he was a movie star, like Clark Gable or Harrison Ford — worked two jobs so they'd have enough money until Bev could start working too. He was a biology teacher at the junior high in Belmont, Massachusetts (we looked it up on Google Earth, once, just to see the building), and then three nights a week he worked as a bartender at a pub in Brighton, which, as Bev explained to Cassie, and Cassie to me, is basically in Boston. Thursdays, Fridays, Saturdays — Cassie even knew which days. Late on a Friday night, when he was driving home from Boston in bad weather, a February night when Cassie was just eleven months old, another car came across the median and hit him head-on. A drunk driver. Bev would tell how she'd fallen asleep and woken at four in the morning with Cassie cozy in the bed beside her, and no Clarke. He hadn't come home, and he didn't answer his cell phone. She wasn't a worrier, so her first thought was that he'd stayed over in Boston at a friend's, which he sometimes did, and she felt annoyed, because it was going to be Saturday and they'd had plans and now everything would be late. She went back to sleep feeling annoyed at Clarke and she woke up again around seven still feeling annoyed and then at 7:30 the police called and she found out that Clarke was dead. All the years since, Bev had told my mother, and my mother had told me, she'd felt guilty about being annoyed, about not thinking the best of him, when of course he would have been home if he could have been — he'd been on his way.

Clarke Burnes was like an angel for Cassie. She believed that he watched over her and kept her safe. She had dreams where they were together, always good dreams, where they toasted marshmallows or rode bikes, or where he tucked her into bed at night and she'd memorize his face, the face she remembered from when she was a baby in her crib. When she was eight, she'd heard his voice in her head — she'd *known* it was his voice, somehow — telling her not to go out onto the ice on Long Pond in January. She was walking the Audubon loop with her mother but had run on ahead and wanted desperately to go sliding; and as she was about to jump off the bank, the voice said, *Stay with me, baby doll. Stay here on the shore*. That's what Cassie said: he'd called her 'baby doll,' and just hearing the words made her feel safe. He was with her; she was never alone. Which was totally different from some cartoon phantom haunting the quarry.

'Sometimes,' she once told me, 'I'm totally sure he's alive. Not just in my mind, but really out there. Like he's just around the corner, waiting for me, for real. Because I can feel him so close by, you know? Like he's with me. Angels,' she'd whispered fiercely, 'are *real*.'

I'd seen his picture: Cassie kept it in a plastic baggie in her underwear drawer, and sometimes slept with it under her pillow. It was strange to me that there weren't pictures of him all over their house, pictures of him and Bev together, or him holding Cassie as a baby, but Cassie explained that her mother's grief had been so intense and so deep that for a long time she couldn't bear to look at photos of Clarke, and had hidden them all. They didn't even have a grave to visit, because he'd been cremated, and Bev told Cassie about their winter trip to the seashore, Cassie not even walking yet, to scatter his ashes in the Atlantic. Flecks had blown back in their faces, Bev told Cassie, and probably they'd swallowed a few. It wasn't disgusting, she said, it was a miracle of nature, that he was always inside them.

Miraculously, that one photo had survived, tucked into the back of the family Bible, where Cassie had found it when she was about seven: she was using the Bible to build a racing run for Matchbox cars and it had fallen out. They'd never spoken about it, although her mother had surely seen it in her underwear drawer — Cassie wasn't trying to hide it.

In truth, it was hard to tell exactly what Clarke Burnes looked like: the photo was from a long time ago and blurry, taken in front of what looked like a barn on a gray fall day. The man in the picture had a square face and floppy blondish hair over one eye, and his hands were stuffed in his jeans pockets. He'd been moving a bit when the shutter snapped, so you couldn't even tell that his eyes were blue (Bev had told Cassie they were); and you couldn't really describe his expression: like he was on the verge of something, in between moments rather than in one. He wore a blue T-shirt with a peace sign on it, and over top a red-and-black plaid flannel shirt. The shirt always seemed to me the most definite thing in the photograph, the only thing you could be absolutely certain you'd recognize, which was strange because it looked like a million other plaid flannel shirts. In the fall, in tiny Royston, you might see half a dozen of those shirts on any given day. I never said that to Cassie — why would I? It wasn't what she needed to hear. So instead when we looked at the photo together, we'd try to pick out which of his features she'd inherited, which blurry bits she carried around in her body.

Knowing all this and how she felt about him, I should never have brought it up the way I did, as if I didn't understand what he meant to her. She didn't mention it again, but it was one of those events that was little and big at the same time.

We made our way home for grilled cheese and chocolate shakes, then we filled a plastic basin and gave each other pedicures until Bev came to pick Cassie up. I painted Union Jacks on her toes — I'd watched a YouTube video on how to do it

— and they came out well except on her baby toes, where the nails were too tiny.

She couldn't do anything nearly so fancy for me because of her hand, so she just painted my toes dark blue and I stuck on little silver star stickers. My feet looked like the night sky.

⋆ ⋆ ⋆

The next day we returned to the quarry. We packed a picnic lunch so we could stay longer, maybe even all day. My mother, in the middle of writing an article, wasn't paying much attention, but I told her we were going for a hike in the woods and might be gone a while.

'Don't go near the highway,' she said, which was absurd, because the quarry was on the other side of town from the highway. 'And take your cell phone in case you need me.'

'You got it.'

'You know you can count on us, Mrs. Robinson,' Cassie said.

We didn't stop at Bell's, and we didn't stop at the Rite Aid, and when we passed the high school, Cassie gave Beckett the finger from too far away for him to see — 'Just a precaution,' she said.

'Like warding off vampires with garlic,' I said.

Turning off the road into the woods, up the trail to the quarry, was like stepping into a dream. Sweat ran down my spine between the hot backpack and my skin, and my fingers, striped red and white, were twice their normal size, but the shade and the rustling leaves made the heat bearable, and the rippling light shot wavery spots of sun onto unexpected patches of bark or mounds of leaves. The vegetation, green- and brown-smelling at the same time, filled our nostrils. The woods were at once very quiet and not quiet at all: things popped or flicked or thudded, birds chirped and hooted, the breeze spoke through the leaves. We stopped to listen, and Cassie pointed out that when a car passed back on the road, it sounded like a great wave at the shore.

As we approached the quarry, we could hear voices and the sound of splashing. Not buoyant kid splashing, boys doing cannonballs, but sedate splashing, and quiet, grown-up voices. Old Mr. Kirschbaum and his wife, we realized as we came near the water's edge. Originally Austrian or something, they were formal and a little scary. He had a pointy gray beard and smoked a pipe — he didn't have the pipe that day — and wore a blazer even in the summertime, so it was surprising to see him in a bathing suit, his saggy old man's bosoms speckled with white hair. His elegant wife, Adele Kirschbaum, who taught piano to the talented kids like May Hwang, wore a black one-piece and an old-fashioned custard-colored bathing cap with a strap under the chin. When we arrived, she was swimming up and down, a careful matron's breaststroke that didn't involve putting her head anywhere near the water. (As Cassie said later, 'What's the crazy cap for, then? A fashion statement?')

Cassie and I hung back in the trees. I started to whisper but Cassie put her finger to her lips.

We both knew that Mr. Kirschbaum would be a stickler for rules — he was old, wasn't he, and, crucially, Austrian — and he'd know that neither of us belonged to the quarry club. My mother had written an article a couple of years before decrying the private membership of what she felt should be public spaces, spaces in nature; so anybody who knew who I was (which the Kirschbaums would, being patients of my dad's) would know that the Robinsons didn't belong. As for Cassie, she just wasn't *the sort*. They'd know that by looking at her. One of those things we were too young to know we knew, but we knew it just the same.

We froze for what seemed like minutes, then Cassie tapped me on the arm and began, with exaggerated steps, to retreat backward into the undergrowth.

'*Around*,' she mouthed, without making a sound. '*Around to the asylum*.'

At first I only got 'around.' I was trying to keep my eyes simultaneously on her, behind me, and on the Kirschbaums ahead, who might hear footsteps, or the splutter of our stifled laughter. But as Cassie said later, 'Couldn't you tell just by *looking* that he'd be deaf? And she had that cap over her ears — probably so she wouldn't have to hear *him*. Because you could tell just by looking that he's an a-hole too.'

Which was mean, but I laughed anyway. Laughter was the point of so many things we did together. Cassie made everything funny, like her giant tiptoeing back toward the road, her silly staring face, holding her forearms up like a kangaroo, her dressed hand a bright-white blob in the muted colors of the forest.

'Better be careful,' she hissed when she thought we were far enough back. 'For all we know, he might be a hunter. Might think my paw is a deer's tail, and shoot.'

'Might,' I said, 'or your hair, for that matter.' How conspicuous she was; how completely she failed to blend in with our surroundings. 'But he won't. More likely to turn us in to Rudy and let that dog eat us for dinner.'

'A dog already ate me for lunch,' Cassie said. 'I don't want to be dinner too.'

We stood for a moment, able to discern, still, the muted sounds of the Kirschbaums talking — it wasn't English they spoke to each other, you could tell without hearing the words — as they continued to slip smoothly through the water.

'What now?' I asked. The backpack containing our lunch stuck moistly to my shirt.

'It's obvious, right? Picnic at the asylum.'

'The asylum?'

'Duh!'

'But I'm so hot.'

'Everything happens for a reason, my mom always says. Asylum first, swim later. They can't be here all afternoon. Do you think that lady sunbathes?'

'But we don't know where the asylum *is*. I don't know if it's such a good idea.'

'Crap, Juju. That's crap. Scaredy-cat. Wriggly Robinson, wriggling out of the fun, afraid of getting in trouble.'

'Am not.'

'Scared of ghosts, are you? Boooo!' She made a taunting face. 'Are you up for it, Scaredy, or do you need to run on home?'

'Whatever else,' I said, 'I'm not a scaredy-cat. Let's go.'

There were no signs. At my insistence we followed the trails rather than setting off blind through the trees. The red-dot trail turned out to be a loop, and brought us back to the quarry on the other side of the parking lot twenty minutes after we left. The Kirschbaums' crimson Prius was still parked between two Norwegian maples. We followed the blue-triangle trail for a while before Cassie protested, 'This one's uphill. Think about it. If we went back out to the main road and followed it to the turn-off that goes down by the asylum, there's no hill between here and there. This can't be right.'

I was tired, and getting hungry. The backpack weighed on me. 'We don't know what we're looking for,' I said. 'Maybe we need to ask one of the older kids and come back another day.'

'Who do you know who's actually *been* there? Not just bragged about it, but been there?'

I shook my head. It was a bit of a myth, like the drowned boy in the quarry. If you drove past the asylum from the road, you couldn't see anything but the long stretch of high stone wall, and the padlocked gates with the sign: no trespassing. What you could see of the drive behind the gates was straggly and overhung with branches, the gravel sprouting waist-high bursts of Queen Anne's lace and goldenrod. It wouldn't have surprised me to learn that nobody we knew had ever really seen the building: it was the sort of thing you wished you'd done, without actually wishing to do it.

'There's only the green trail left,' Cassie said. 'I vote we go back to the parking lot, take the green trail, and then we'll see.'

'I vote we eat.'

'It's not like you're not going to *get* your lunch. I'm just suggesting you try harder for it.'

Cassie could be affectionate and scornful at the same time, and I always felt that if I wasn't careful, the scorn might win out. So we returned to the parking lot and set off down the green-square trail. The Prius was still there.

⋆ ⋆ ⋆

The green trail proved messier and more confusing than the other two — fewer unchanging rocks, more diverse foliage, and muckier too. Pretty soon we were picking our way alongside a brook. Not especially large, the brook made a pleasing gurgly sound. A ribbon of clear water in a small gully, passing over piles of debris and winding blithely around others, it looked as though, like Miss Buono, our social studies teacher, it might vary a lot in size depending on the season. I made this point to Cassie, and then said, 'Right now, it's August, and both the stream and Miss B are in bikini season: skimpy.' Which made Cassie laugh — there's something hilarious about the word 'skimpy,' if you repeat it over and over. But she couldn't resist saying, 'No matter what the season, Buono's butt is *big*.' And we were snickering about Miss B's butt when Cassie pointed out a flattened log across the stream, upon which someone had piled three large, flat stones.

'What's that then?'

'Not the path. The next green square is on that tree up there.'

'It's not *the* path, but it's *a* path.' If you looked on the other side of the stream you could pick out the traces of a path winding off through the woods. Not marked, but worn, and not worn only by a single set of feet. It looked like nobody'd been down it in a while, but I could tell that excited Cassie all the more.

'I'm sure that's it,' she said.

The forest lay very still.

'Who put the stones, do you think?'

'Who cares?' Cassie replied. 'They've been there for ages. Look — moss.' The little pile of stones was dotted with near-luminous lichen, in starburst patterns.

'Okay. Let's go.' I stepped onto the log, which gave slightly beneath me, soft and rotted by damp. It didn't break.

'For real?' Cassie's eyes glittered, and it occurred to me that all along she'd expected me to stop us. She'd goaded and teased me, made out like I was a wimp; but she also relied on me to keep us safe.

'For real,' I said.

The path, such as it was, would seem to come and go, and the greenery overhead became more dense, the sun more obscured, as if we were going ever deeper into the woods. I tried to trace a mental map — we turned right at the broad rotted stump, we bore left where the two maple trunks had grown intertwined, we kept the water behind our left ears and its gurgly sound came near, and retreated, and came again. I knew I'd have to reverse these signs on the return (turn *left* at the rotted stump), and worried that I'd get muddled. I even pulled some pages from the little notebook in my pack and impaled them on branches along the way — like Cassie's white mitt, they'd stand out, I thought, in the swimmy green.

⋆ ⋆ ⋆

The sad building loomed enormous. We crested the hillock, toward the light, and at first could see nothing but more sky down the other side. A hundred yards down the slope, we broke out of the trees, into what had obviously been a large lawn, a field now, its long grasses swaying in the hot sun, the desperate saw of crickets all around. Wildflowers were scattered through the grasses — flashes of pink, purple, and orange in the bleached ripples: coneflowers, cosmos, calendula, coreopsis. And the air, so long moist between the trees, smelled dry, a late-summer smell of safety.

The long grassy stretch — broken here and there by wispy saplings — ended in steps leading to a stone patio. We'd come up the back. Instead of the circular drive, the portico and the garages, we were confronted by banks of darkened windows, like eyes in the three-story, U-shaped brick facade, as if the building were an almost human monster. On the ground floor, on the wings at either side, we could see brown-painted metal doors. But in the middle of the *U* — its basin, if you will — stretched a span of French windows giving onto a terrace, and there, just for a moment, you could picture the rich man's residence the house had originally been: you could imagine the French doors ajar, curtains fluttering in the breeze, on the terrace a few tables shaded by large parasols, and a house party of elegant men and women drifting, holding china teacups or smoking cigars. Then you noticed the heavy padlocked chain that ran through the doors' institutional bars, rusty but still newer than the general disintegration at first suggested. Some poorly scrubbed blue graffiti stretched along one wall. We could make out GO CAVALIERS — our high school ice hockey team — and MOTHERFUCKERS.

'Lunchtime,' I said. When we reached the patio — strewn not only with leaves but with shards of glass and strips of roof tile, with crushed beer cans and cigarette butts — I slapped myself down on the top step, the house behind me and the hairy green forest we'd come out of in front of me, and I opened the backpack on the smutty stone ledge. I laid out the tea towel from my mother's clean kitchen, and on it I placed the items one by one: the carrot and cucumber sticks; the hard-boiled eggs with their little sealed packets of salt filched from diners;

the sandwiches wrapped in foil; the Camelbak of lemonade, the one of iced tea, their ice cubes long melted after our trek.

While we ate, Cassie stalked the terrace, squinting in at the windows, grasping her sandwich with both hands in her distinctive way, made slightly comical by the fact that one hand was a gauzy paw.

⋆ ⋆ ⋆

What did we know about the asylum? Not much. It had been built at the turn of the last century by a textile merchant named Ebenezer Otis, to house his collection of Asian art. His mills were in Lowell, his city house was on Commonwealth Avenue in Boston; but this, outside Royston, was his country estate. The fortune was lost in the Crash of '29, and the house and the art had to be sold. Some giant vases, ivory dragons, and lacquered chests were acquired by the Peabody Essex Museum, where a couple are even on display.

The state ended up buying the property at a discount price — where were the Otis descendants today? In condos on the outskirts of Gloucester? — and after leaving it empty a few lean years, they converted it to a women's mental asylum, the Bonnybrook. I guess there was that brook, at least. It housed up to forty-five women at a time, stricken with a gamut of complaints — depression, mania, schizophrenia, addiction. According to the official records, many got better and went back to their real lives.

Time passed, views changed, laws and funding with them. By the late 1980s it was seen as unsalvageable, and by '93, the Bonnybrook was shuttered, forgotten. Part of the same parcel of land as the quarry, it was sold to a consortium that then couldn't agree on its fate — whether to refit it as apartments, or restore it as a mansion hotel. Word was, there'd been a dragging lawsuit. It had been padlocked and empty longer than I'd been alive.

I imagined that the building carried the sadness of the women who'd been trapped there, the anorexic teenagers and the young mothers who heard voices and the old women shattered past repair by their tragedies. I didn't *see* them — there was no visible mass of ghosts peering out of the hollowed windows — but I couldn't help but feel they marked the territory.

Cassie didn't feel that way at all — quite the opposite. She wouldn't be put off. I trailed after her as she walked the perimeter and climbed a rickety fire escape, fruitlessly rattling the windows in their frames on each floor.

When we reached the front of the house, its broad circular drive long overgrown and its crumbling stables off to one side, she counted the entrances — six ground-floor windows, three visible doors — and divided them between us. As I tugged half-heartedly at a bolted knob, I heard the tinkle of glass breaking. I looked to see Cassie curiously bent, her ear against a window and her paw to the frame, her good arm stuck up inside its shattered pane like she was birthing a calf.

'Are you fucking insane?'

She didn't turn her head. Her tongue stuck out between tight lips, the way it did when she concentrated in math class, but she paused long enough to say, 'It's going to work, Juju. I'm going to get it.' And after a minute more of trying, 'I didn't break the window, you know. It was already broken. I just knocked the bits sticking out along the edges.'

'Tell that to the jury.'

'Christ, what's wrong with you?' She stuck her tongue out again, twisted and fiddled. And paused again. 'Can't you see this could be *ours*? Our own world, a *real* world, that we found, and we made, and we kept? Our real secret?'

When she put it that way, I suddenly understood. The mansion looked different, no longer a house of sorrows, or a hideout for drunk hockey players from the high school, or a possible flophouse for escapees from the penitentiary up the highway. I could see it: the Bonnybrook as a magical place we could invent, the two of us, and have as ours, the way we'd thought of it before I saw it, a stage for our best imaginary adventures. Like seeing the hot sun and the crickets as a gift, like the bright wildflowers, instead of as a sinister menace. Like we had the power — Cassie and I, the two of us, twelve years old — to make anything into what we wanted it to be.

I said, 'Let me try. My arm is longer.' Cassie and I looked at each other, almost smiling but not, a kind of mutual *Mona Lisa* look. She extricated her good arm, careful not to nick herself on any protruding fragments, straightened and stepped away, crunching broken glass on the gravel as she went.

I took Cassie's place and folded myself like a strange origami, my cheek pressed against an unbroken pane and my neck stretched flat along the rib of the window, and my left arm, my writing arm — I always thought, faintly guiltily, my better arm — up inside the house, squirming and reaching.

The air inside the house was cooler, fresh on my skin. I could feel the lock, but I wasn't able to reach quite high enough to flick it from one side to the other.

Cassie started to laugh.

'What?'

'Did I look like that?' She made a crazy face.

'It's *hard*.'

'You don't need to tell me.' She laughed again, light in her bird bones like the wind in the grass.

'It's not going to work.' My sweat left a film on the window when I pulled away.

'It's got to work,' Cassie said. 'We're going in.'

I peered in the window. We stood outside a big common room, with fancy moldings on the ceiling and wainscoting waist high. The plaster was crumbling and in places mold bloomed, giant flower paintings along the walls. A dozen folding chairs stood stacked in rows against the far wall and old paint cans rusted in piles next to a swing door. The air in the gloom was hazed with dust, and the floor — once fancy parquet, the kind you might find in a ballroom — was strewn with debris, with plaster crumbs and plastic bottles and what looked like a layer of dried mud. From the ceiling hung two wagon-wheel chandeliers, ugly, clunky things surely acquired cheaply to replace whatever had originally been in the house. A long buffet bar extended along the far wall next to the chairs: the dining hall.

Cupping my eyes against the window, I could almost see the institutional room with its stacks of damp fake-wood trays, and stringy-haired, shiftless girls barely older than me lined up before steaming vats of baked beans and soggy broccoli, some hideous perversion of summer camp, where you didn't get any care packages and nobody came to take you home.

I could see too the parquet sparkling beneath the crystal chandeliers that once had hung from their sunburst moldings, and the flickering wall sconces along the walls, this diffuse and inconstant light illuminating, again, the faces of girls — and boys — not so much older than me, but in a different life, one of spangled baubles and velvet dresses, the young men in dinner jackets, a jazz band installed in the room's back right corner where, I could swear, a dais had been placed precisely for them. Instead of the plastic-paneled buffet bar with its red heat lamps, long, cloth-covered tables bore silver tureens of punch, and pyramids of petits fours and chocolate strawberries, and behind these stood a quiet row of young men and women in dark uniforms — the staff, attending to every whim of the North Shore's gilded youth.

Just a big abandoned room, almost empty, but

like Cassie, I understood now that we had to go in. I suggested breaking the windowpane above the broken one. That would put the window latch firmly in my fingers.

We knew we were crossing a line. This went further than trying a joint with Devon Macintyre down in the cemetery at Luna's end-of-school party back in June; or than Cassie filching a twenty from her mother's wallet to buy a jumbo bag of Skittles and Big Gulps of Coke at the multiplex, when Bev had expressly forbidden us to. This was law-breaking: the sign on the gate out at the road did say NO TRESPASSING: TRESPASSERS WILL BE PROSECUTED, and we were already trespassing and were about not just to *enter* but to *break and enter*. But it felt *necessary*, like we didn't really have a choice.

I made Cassie stand far back while I broke the window, because I didn't want any glass to bounce up and hit her, and I didn't want any fragments to get in her bandage. She stood by with the otherworldly look she'd worn when we crossed the field. A look, if you like, of destiny.

* * *

When we'd climbed through the opened window Cassie whooped — a testing sort of whoop, louder at the end, that echoed in the hollow room. Then she spun in circles, arms outstretched, leaving swirling marks along the dusty floor, whooping the whole time. I fussed about a glass cut along my elbow — not deep, but I squeezed out a little rivulet of blood that I wiped with my finger and sucked. My mother always told me that if you don't have disinfectant, you want to make sure the cut bleeds cleanly, to wash the germs out. So that's what I did first.

We pushed the swinging door to check out the kitchens: two big rectangular rooms, laid end to end, with black-and-white checkerboard flooring like at my house, but miles of it, like something out of *Alice in Wonderland*; and rows of stainless-steel counters dulled by years of filth. Cassie tried the taps at one of the industrial sinks, but nothing came out, which was just as well, as it would have flushed the complex spider's web spun across the sink itself. We opened some cabinet doors — not metal but painted wood, or once-painted wood, and when we left them open the doors dangled drunkenly on their hinges — but found nothing except a clutch of stiffened paintbrushes and an ancient empty gallon plastic Coke bottle.

'People have been here.' Cassie pointed to some sticky rings in the dust on one of the countertops. 'Before us.'

'Not for a long time.'

'Do you think the Coke is from when they moved everything out, twenty years ago? Or from last year, when, say, DeLouis Runyon was hiding out here?' DeLouis Runyon was a high school junior from Worcester, famous because he beat up his math teacher, also his hockey coach, and ran away before the cops got him. He was missing for seventy-two hours and then turned himself in. Nobody knew where he'd been exactly, or they weren't saying. But he hadn't been at the Bonnybrook — we were too far from Worcester. Most likely he'd been in his girlfriend's garage.

'Last year? I doubt it. But maybe not so long as twenty years. Remember the chains on the doors at the back? They're newer than that. So maybe they had a problem with people, you know, coming in a while back, like five years or ten, and put the locks on then.'

We both considered the crazy number of days in which this building had stood empty, how on any one of them — far more days than either of us had been alive, though not quite as many as all of our days put together — in this house anything could have happened; and most strangely of all, how on most of those days, even *almost all* of those days, nothing had. Sure, kids like us had broken in before, and hung out drinking on the patio, and maybe a few times some nut had spent a night here. Maybe even half a dozen nights. Imagine someone had even lived in the Bonnybrook for a month: that would still leave seventeen years and eleven months, well over six thousand days and nights of total silence, a once-human habitation uninhabited, given over instead to spiders and chipmunks and robins and potentially the occasional fox. It overwhelmed, in the way the night sky overwhelms when you lie on your back in the grass and stare at it, at all the tiny points of light, and imagine the unimaginable distances between those stars and Earth, and how long even the light has taken to get to your eye, so long that maybe the star that emitted that light is already, in actuality, long gone.

'I vote we see upstairs first,' Cassie said.

In the front hallway, we peered up the staircase at the big stained-glass window with its lilies in a vase and crimson tracery, only a few panes knocked in, their bright fragments scattered on the wood floor. Someone had pulled up boards, leaving rutted gaps underfoot; but the newel post at the bottom of the stairs had proven too sturdy for the thieves — its carved finial was the size of my head, a great once-polished ball of patterned flowers and vines, a vinery traced all up the banister and the length of the balustrades as well.

'Can't you see the grand ladies coming down?' Cassie breathed at my ear. 'In their evening dresses?'

'Sure I can,' I said, and it was true, I could. 'And right behind them, do you see the crazy girls in blue smocks with their hair sticking up anyhow and wild eyes? Do you see them too?' I gave a great cackling laugh that resounded up the stairwell, an evil madwoman's laugh. 'That's the noise they're making — can you hear it? It's wicked loud.'

'Don't.' Cassie pressed my arm. We both looked up the stairs at the dust motes drifting in a shaft of sun across the landing. We could feel them with us — I knew she did just as much as I; and they too were our sisters. 'Don't.'

To be in that ruin with Cassie — it was such a particular feeling that I have had nowhere else. If ever I have it again, I will recognize it, like a long-lost scent, and that afternoon and the ones that followed will return to me, in all their visceral intensity. The Bonnybrook was at once the most unlikely, vivid experience of our lives up till then, and like a dream — a dream, miraculously, that Cassie and I dreamed in tandem, touching, hearing, and feeling together. The asylum was darkened by the traces of its pasts; made titillating, even scary, by its silences — but made safer too by our sharing it. Being in the Bonnybrook was like being inside both Cassie's head and my own, as if we had one mind and could roam its limits together, inventing stories and making ourselves as we wanted them to be.

* * *

It took us almost half an hour to get back to the quarry parking lot, walking at a good pace, sweating all over again. The Kirschbaums were nowhere in sight, and it was too early for the after-work swimmers. The quarry lay still as a plate, the water black in the shadows. I lobbied again for a swim, and although Cassie wasn't having it — what good was the water to her mittened paw? — she grudgingly agreed to wait, to let me dive in for just a minute.

I stripped to my panties and bra — one I really liked a lot, with a neon-green-and-brown leopard pattern and some neon lacy trim — and I plunged off the rocks without even dipping in a toe. The smooth cool of it came as a total surprise to my body, a shock, and my swift stroke across the breadth of the quarry made my nerves tingle like sparklers.

Cassie dangled her feet, her face turned up to the sky and her eyes shut, like she was praying, and when I paused, treading water, against the far bank, and looked at her, she glowed, tiny, fragile, in the dappled late-afternoon light.

* * *

After that, Cassie and I went every day to the asylum. We packed our picnic, hiked through town, and then through the woods, along the green trail over the brook, past the cairn of lichened stones, up the hill and over it into the field of flowers, to the manor. The hardest thing was not telling my mother. I'd never been in the midst of anything extraordinary and kept it hidden. I'd told her when Jake Brenner tried to make out with me when we slow-danced at Hester Lee's party in the sixth grade. I'd told her when Andrew Dray brought weed to Cassie's church youth group's summer luau. I'd told her about my yearlong crush on Peter Oundle. She knew how to say the right thing and not pry, to wait for me to want to talk and let me explain what mattered without passing judgment.

It wasn't hard for Cassie, who never confided in her mother. Bev Burnes wasn't reliable; she was moody and weird in spite of her perma-smiles, and even if she seemed cool about something, it didn't mean she'd stay cool with it, and weeks or even months later she could throw it back in Cassie's face, or blab like it was nothing. Cassie had learned the hard way not to trust her mother.

★ ★ ★

We ventured daily up the grand staircase to long corridors of almost identical rooms, in which torn blinds still dangled at the cracked and smeary windows, or in which sinks encrusted with desiccated black slime hung askew from the walls, their taps useless. A few cells had kept their metal bedsteads, long stripped of mattresses, slats like broken keys, legs buckled, rusted into some sort of dinosaur artwork. We marveled at the occasional bursts of bright mold across a bedroom wall — orange, watermelon, lime — where seeping damp had encouraged a new life form. We wanted to take photographs — my new cell phone, a birthday present, could take pretty good pictures — but we knew better.

'No evidence,' I warned as we pored over the mildew flowers in their resplendent bloom, and Cassie grabbed at my backpack, to show she wanted my phone. 'We can't leave any evidence, anywhere.'

She stopped, blinked, about to protest, and then nodded. 'No evidence,' she whispered back at me solemnly, then laughed. 'It's no mistake that you get all A's, Juju my friend. The girl thinks ahead.' If my mother found photos of the asylum on my phone, we'd be grounded for weeks. We had to do this old-style. The way it had been for centuries before our time: no one must know.

We explored what had been the lockdown ward — the Isolation Ward, we called it, to ourselves — the wing that stretched out above the dining room, behind two strong metal doors that no longer shut properly, a corridor along which each cell had its own reinforced door with a little sliding window, like in prison, and within each bedroom, the windows squinted out small and high and barred, with chicken-wire mesh in the glass behind the bars.

'This is where they put the real loonies,' Cassie said.

'How crazy did you have to be, I wonder. What kind of crazy?'

'And if there were enough people who were that kind of crazy to fill up all these rooms' — there were about fifteen of these little cells along that forlorn corridor — 'then where did they go?'

I didn't have a clue. In twenty years, they couldn't all have died — but even if they had, the world wasn't getting any less crazy. So the dying generation of crazies was being replaced all the time by new crazies, a rolling population of lunatics as constant as the tides. Unless it wasn't individuals that changed but society itself: they changed the laws, they closed the asylums, and suddenly the crazies weren't crazy anymore. Maybe when society changed it was decided, somehow, that they never *had* been crazy; it had all been a category mistake.

What would it be like to have been locked up in one of those cells for weeks or months or even years, only to discover that you'd never really been a lunatic at all, and could just as easily — if only the world had been a bit different — have been home in your bedroom all along?

That would mean that you couldn't be sure about things. Better to believe that sane people were sane and crazy people were crazy and you could put the two types of people on opposite sides of a wall and keep them separate, clean and tidy. Without that, where did the lunatics go? Where had they gone? Were they among us? Were they us?

* * *

The kitchens, the storerooms, the dining rooms, the bedrooms, the lounges, the bathrooms — those rows of bleak open shower stalls, with their stained puce tile and twisted shower heads like Cyclops eyes — the echoey hallways, the staff quarters somehow cozier than the rest even after almost twenty years of decay, rooms that still had the moldings and trim, the built-in shelves and wainscoting of the original mansion, the floors still wooden rather than tiled — all of these corners we charted, together, sometimes shouting loudly to hide our fear, sometimes gripping each other by the arm and walking on tiptoe, like when we heard a squirrel foraging and thought it was a person, or the ghost of a person.

Together Cassie and I confronted the asylum and our terror of it, and by the end of the third afternoon, it felt familiar, almost familial, and we ran in the corridors, our feet slapping, and laughed and called out and even parted company — we could, we did, on that third afternoon, *play*, as we'd initially planned, and she pretended to be the young lady of the manor, and I was her suitor, and she disappeared upstairs and I gallantly pursued her with rhyming couplets, an eligible bachelor of yore come calling, until she advanced coyly to lean over the banister and I lured her down to the lobby with my blandishments. Or again: I was a psycho, completely off my head, unable to remember who I was or where I was from, estranged from myself and a prisoner in Room 7 of the Isolation Ward, where — convincingly, I thought — I curled on the floor in a ball and rocked and wailed so loudly that Cassie could find me, setting off from the lobby in an elaborate version of hide-and-seek, and when she found me, she was my long-lost sister, and she sat beside me and held my hand, and by singing our favorite songs brought me back to myself, recalling to me our shared childhood and our dog, Sheba, and our parents, CIA agents tragically killed on the same mission that had come close to exterminating me, the trauma of which had stolen my memory entire, and left me floating alone and delirious on a raft off the coast of Maine, which was how I came to be here at the Bonnybrook, just a few miles from my beloved childhood home, to which Cassie would now safely return me.

We'd done the Greek myths in school that year, so we knew the basics, and we acted out some of those too. She was Jocasta; I, Oedipus. I was Agamemnon; she, Clytemnestra. She, Heracles to my Deianeira.

The time came that we felt free, running and shouting as if we owned the place. So we were lucky to be up in the wards when Rudy pulled up the drive in his truck one early afternoon, with Bessie in the flatbed, her paws up on the side and nose to the wind, barking. Her barking alerted us; we pulled ourselves to standing and peered from either side of the window in our chosen room (Number 7, with a useless black sink, in which we'd piled wildflowers picked in the field), looking down at the tops of their heads. Bessie knew we were there. She may even have known where. I could have sworn she pricked her ears and glanced up at me, paused for a second in the crazed tattoo of her barks. But Rudy was lazy, or tired — the air so hot and humid — and simply rolled down the window so Bessie could hear him yell at her. He told her to 'shut the fuck up': 'Nobody's interested in your goddamn squirrels.'

Along with his shouting and Bessie's barking, we could hear the thud of loud '80s music — Bruce Springsteen, maybe? Something my dad liked — and I knew Rudy was in his own world, not in the real world, maybe imagining he was still young and had all his teeth, when he drove a girl around maybe, if he ever did, with that same music blaring. And because he could see the girl, and see his youthful self, and hear his youth in the melody, there was no way he'd see the decay and detritus that was really in front of his eyes.

Still, we felt shaky long after he drove back down the driveway and disappeared, raising dust off the gravel, Bessie still yammering full bore in the back. We stopped shouting after that, and stopped clattering. If Rudy could appear out of the blue — we hadn't heard him coming — then anybody else could too. Bit by bit the ghosts of former inmates and escaped convicts and the nastier elements of the Cavaliers hockey team slipped back into our minds, and in the next hour the Bonnybrook became frightening again, as it had been when first we approached it. Our games stopped being fun, and we packed up our stuff early to head out, subdued, muttering to each other about the thunderstorms forecast for later.

The next day, Friday, it rained heavily. Bev dropped Cassie off with a particular plump fuss and flurry — 'I've got to run. I'm due at Abe Peterson's and he won't get his morphine till I get there. The night nurse missed her last round, so he's been without since midnight. And it's bone cancer. Imagine that, would you?'

'I'd rather not,' my mother replied, shepherding Cassie in and Bev back out the door. Later, at the dinner table, she said, 'Why, if she was in such a hurry, did she even get out of the car? To come rain in our front hall for a bit?'

My dad smiled, weighing his quinoa and cranberry on his fork. 'Bev likes a show,' he said. 'She doesn't think it happened if nobody was there to see it.'

This sounded true, and made me wonder what other traits that sort of person might have. It made me wonder whether I was that sort of person myself: I always liked to imagine an audience. When I wrote in my diary, I couldn't imagine that the only person who would read it was me; but the whole point of a diary was to record the things you didn't want anybody else to know. Maybe, I sometimes thought, the other reader was simply your older self, the same you, changed by time. This bothered me too, because what was a self, a person, if she could be so changed — as changed as an abandoned building, say? What could we rely on then, besides the rocks in the quarry?

But when Cassie arrived, her near-white hair dripping on her shoulders from the short distance between the Honda and the house, her white bandaged paw aloft, I was preoccupied instead with whether we should bake banana bread or chocolate-chip cookies, whether we should watch a comedy or an action movie, and whether, later, we'd weave friendship bracelets or write a play.

The next Monday morning early, we had a call from Marj, who managed in her way to make tenderness seem businesslike, and who said she'd thought it over and knew how sorry we must be about what happened, and would Cassie and I like to come back for the rest of the month to help out with the cats — only ever the cats, mind you — because that might give everyone a chance to feel better about the whole sad story. She'd called Bev and Cassie first, I discovered later, and Bev had already said yes, which made it easy, even necessary, for my mother to say yes also. So on Monday afternoon, that very day, we were back in our smocks in the stinky, chilled cat room at the animal shelter, up to our gloved elbows in turd-filled litter and swooning over the kittens, Xena and Electra, we would take home.

⋆ ⋆ ⋆

From there, the last stretch of the summer unspooled like thread off a bobbin. We kept meaning to return one more time to the Bonnybrook, but there was always a reason not to. Cassie's dressing came off, her hand scarred but fully functioning. We returned to the Saghafis' pool with its synthetic blue water as if the quarry had never called to us, had never been. We made plans for the fall; we went back-to-school shopping; we slept sanely in our beds, and got on with things.

Only months later, we heard that the property had been sold on, that the developers who'd bought it were lobbying at the State House in Boston to build condos around the original mansion. We heard too that the new people had properly sealed the perimeter with barbed-wire fence, including on the trail through the woods from the quarry.

Then, and for all sorts of reasons, our Bonnybrook days, our shared dream, came to seem like something that might never really have happened. And once Cassie and I came unstuck, neither of us had anyone to remind us it was true.

PART TWO

My mother assures me that it happens to everyone, sooner or later, for reasons more or less identifiable; everyone loses a best friend at some point. Not in the 'she moved to Tucson' sense, but in the sense that 'we grew apart.'

I, who pride myself on seeing things, can't even now properly sort out what happened. Cassie had her version, though she never told it to me, and when, much later, I asked her outright ('What happened to us?' is how I put it, which seemed more neutral than I felt) she looked at me a long time — a look I'd describe as 'hurt,' though I was the one who'd been wronged, surely? — and shook her head slightly. When I gave her a chance to explain, that was the best she could do.

Seventh grade is difficult for most. My parents said it was the time of life they'd least like to live again, which wasn't helpful, as I had no choice but to live it. But seventh grade is differently difficult for each person. For Zach Filkins, it was difficult because they didn't have a middle school math class challenging enough for him and he had to go over to the high school to join the advanced freshmen. On the other hand, Zach wasn't interested in going to the middle school prom, so didn't ask anyone, and didn't have to contemplate the possibility of rejection. Whereas Brent O'Connor — a nice guy, but in seventh grade he still didn't break five feet — had to brave the humiliation of being turned down for the dance by three girls, one of whom was me (I was already 5′6″ — it was impossible). Then there was the slightly different challenge of being Alicia Homans, the fourth girl he asked, who knew it, but who accepted cheerfully and held her head as high as if she'd been his first choice.

There are the social struggles, and the agonies and embarrassments of puberty (I won't forget the mixture of triumph and pity I felt when Bridget Mulvaney flounced down the corridor tossing her famous auburn curls, with a period stain the size of a saucer on her purple gypsy skirt), and the weight of the world that falls upon each of us in varying degrees, as we finally relinquish childhood's clouds of glory to live, ever after, in our earthly realm.

In seventh grade, Jude Robben lived up to his name and was arrested for shoplifting a camera from Walmart. Andrew Dray got a caution from his law-enforcement uncle for weed smoking and small-time dealing. Rumor had it that Stacey Bilic gave blow jobs to half a dozen guys in one night at Tessa Rubin's party in late May of that year, and the struggle for Stacey was that it didn't matter whether the rumor was true. There was no point loudly denying it, because that meant no more as a truth or a falsehood than did the original story: in seventh grade, we moved suddenly into a world of adult actions and of adult conjecture.

It was also a world of adult consciousness, with all the strangeness that implies. Like: my mother's story about Cassie and me is that our paths, always destined to diverge, simply took their natural course. It was a given, for example, that I'd eventually go to college. Because my parents assumed I would, but also because I wanted to, because I was good at school and proud of it and couldn't imagine not going on to more school after school. Even when I'd dreamed of being a pop star, I imagined going to NYU or UCLA in between performances.

But Cassie's mother hadn't gone to college for the pleasure of learning. She'd studied nursing only later, in her midtwenties, right before she had Cassie. She'd left school at eighteen and worked as a waitress, and then in the hat and glove department at Macy's, apparently — which always surprised me, because I thought of department-store staff as tidy and elegant.

Cassie wasn't especially good at school, and she didn't like it enough to work at it, and by seventh grade this had consequences. We'd left the elementary for the middle school, up Route 29, not far from the animal shelter. For those of us from Royston, middle school was just two years, because Royston Elementary had a sixth grade; but a lot of the other kids from neighboring towns had already been there a year. The school building, gray concrete unlike our cozy old Victorian elementary school downtown, squatted in an enormous parking lot between two strip malls. Its Astroturf fields glowed curiously green in all seasons; but mostly we lived in the locker-lined, windowless hallways, all of us lumpy and greasy in the fluorescence. Kids from the other towns seemed bigger and older than the kids we knew. Whereas before school had felt like a cheerful dysfunctional family — we'd known most of our classmates all our lives — now it felt like a parade ground, a theater of strange performances. Suddenly, we didn't share the same schedules, or teachers, or classrooms; scattered, we didn't necessarily even arrive or leave together. Cassie and I were pushed apart by bureaucracy.

I got put in advanced math and advanced English and while the school didn't technically have an advanced history class, Cassie and I were in different sections, and mysteriously she was in with the troublemakers like Stacey Bilic and Andrew Dray, while I was in with May Hwang and Zach Filkins and Angie Pitts, the daughter of Mr. Pitts, the high school AP history teacher. Cassie and I were together only for PE and orchestra, where she played the flute and I played the cello and we sat on opposite sides of the room anyhow.

That's what my mother felt happened, and maybe partly she was right. But I blamed the new girl from two towns over, Delia Vosul, whom I quickly took to calling the Evil Morsel. At first Cassie laughed and we made fun of Delia together — she had orangey-blond blow-dried hair, bulging push-up bras and shiny lip gloss, and a way of glancing at boys out of the corner of her sleepy almond eye as if she were Sofia Vergara, starring in a TV show invisible to anyone but herself.

But Delia and Cassie had history and math

and English together, and by the beginning of October they had 'study dates,' which, as I said to my mom, seemed mostly to involve going to Rite Aid. Cassie tried to tell me that actually Delia was really nice — and funny, she said she was funny, when anyone could tell the girl had the sense of humor of a brick. Then it turned out that Delia liked to sing, that she too wanted to be a pop star, and planned to audition for the spring musical, though when she sang Adele in the cafeteria and Cassie, admiring, flashed her gap-toothed grin, her voice was thin and raspy and she sang flat and couldn't tell. Mr. Montgomery, the music teacher, apparently couldn't tell either, because he gave Delia the solo part in the chorus, which we were to perform at the holiday assembly in December. I probably shouldn't have told Cassie that Montgomery only wanted to jump Delia's bones; but I did. In the old days, Cassie would have agreed with me or at least she would have laughed; but in thrall to Delia, she just bit her lip and looked away.

So it wasn't such a surprise when I asked Cassie what we should dress up as for Halloween, and she said she wasn't going trick-or-treating, she was going to spend the evening watching horror movies at Delia's house. I'd discover only later that this was actually a boy-girl party, complete with Truth or Dare and Spin the Bottle, involving older kids. It constituted the Evil Morsel's successful bid for cool. And Cassie's, for that matter, even though she'd always made fun of those things. There were, I found out, just ten kids: five girls and five boys, one of them Peter Oundle from the year above, whom Cassie started dating that very night and would ditch before Christmas, even though she knew I'd liked him for ages.

⋆ ⋆ ⋆

I couldn't help feeling she'd started going out with Peter Oundle just to hurt my feelings. She'd always said she couldn't see the attraction. Maybe Delia the Evil had told her Oundle was desirable, and it wasn't about me at all. Or maybe it was about how into her he was; because according to Cassie (though I couldn't decide if I believed her), Peter confessed that he'd had a crush on her since we were all kids. Whatever her reason for saying yes when he asked if he could kiss her, it stung. We didn't fight outright — I couldn't risk it — but we became stiff with each other. We stepped through the looking glass into a world all of fake friendliness, where Cassie would give me a broad smile when she saw me — but not too big, do you see? Like the parody of her old smile; and I would smile too, although it felt like a grimace, and I was sure everyone around us, and Cassie most of all, could see the sham of it. But she wasn't letting on; she would smile and smile and be a villain, and I, who felt like a Catholic light-up statuette of Mary with a bleeding heart, would stand there bleeding, invisibly bleeding out, holding my lunch tray with May Hwang at my elbow and a grin on my face.

She fell hard for the Evil Morsel. If I'd held my tongue, if I'd tried harder — not even to be friends with Delia, but maybe just uncritically to let Cassie be friends with her — maybe then? I'm not convinced, but maybe. As it was, I'd shown my hand from the beginning. I'd called the girl Evil Morsel, for God's sake. There was no way back from that.

* * *

That September Bev too fell in love. I didn't know, at first. Strange, blowsy Bev, with her sweet-smelling honey hair and her flowy skirts, who seemed even further removed from romance than my own parents, as far gone into the realm of sexlessness as Nino Zeppala, the woodshop teacher with the leather vest and steampunk beard — Bev fell in love with a man at her Bible study group. Bev fell in love with Dr. Anders Shute.

Now of course I wonder whether they first met at the hospital in Haverhill when Cassie went to get her bandage off. I don't recall Cassie saying that she'd seen Dr. Shute that late August day; but that doesn't mean it didn't happen. Because it seemed a pretty big coincidence that he'd join the Bible study that fall, just out of the blue. Bev had been a part of it for years already then — Alpha Group potlucks and scripture analysis with Pastor Phil from their church, a part of Bev's life that Cassie rolled her eyes over and wanted nothing to do with, always on Tuesday evenings at the same time as Cassie's youth group, which Cassie tolerated because there were a couple of plausible-looking guys.

I don't know how long it was, exactly, before Cassie became aware of Dr. Shute in the hallways of the church — mixing powdered mashed potatoes or frying sausages in the church kitchen, arranging the circle of puffed-seat folding chairs in the community hall before meeting. How long before she knew he was there at all, and how long before she realized that her mother made googly eyes at him and that he, even in his wanness, responded? And what does it tell you that I didn't know until Thanksgiving, when Bev called up my mother to invite us all over to their house for turkey — which had never happened before, although they'd been a few times to our house, in quiet years, the two of them? And when my mother said thanks, but we had my grandparents and my father's brother's family coming to town, Bev said, well how about just for some pie and coffee then, even afterward, because there's someone special I'd like you to meet. My mother agreed we'd stop by for pie, even though she said to me she knew we wouldn't want any, seeing as Grandma Robinson's specialty was pie — pecan, blueberry, strawberry-rhubarb — and we'd be stuffed to the gills by five o'clock.

I felt awkward — and that was before I knew about Dr. Shute. In all the years, my dad had never spent time at the Burneses', and my mom only for a chat or a cup of tea when picking me up or dropping me off. Cassie and I didn't hang out at all, by then — 'Wait, and it will change,' my mother said; or else, 'Growing pains! Growing pains!' as though once we'd all reached some full-size state, fully boobed and menstruating and hormonally rebalanced, Cassie and I would fall back into the rhythms of our friendship as if the Evil Morsel had never existed. We rarely sat together on the bus, and if my mother or Bev picked us up, we ran to the car from different ends of the school steps, and the grown-up kept conversation going on the ride home. I pointed this out and my mother seemed not quite to believe me; but she always had the radio on in the background, so there was never any real silence, and maybe she couldn't tell how it was.

After school, Cassie was often with Peter and Delia and Delia's boyfriend, Arturo, in the eighth grade like Peter, a double-date of cool kids cuddling against the wall; while I stood out on the steps with my backpack at my feet and my headphones on, listening to retro stuff, Adele or Duffy, looking out into the traffic, as if I were in a hurry. I had other friends, but I'd lost the friend I loved best, and had loved without thinking for as long as I could remember, and it seemed absolutely essential not to appear to care.

(Here's another thing I couldn't quite figure out: I *was* full-sized, as was Delia too. I didn't flaunt them like she did, but I had boobs and hips, and by October I had my period too. Whereas Cassie still looked like a kid, tiny and all bones, her jeans from the kids' department. I couldn't fathom how Peter would choose *her*, would want to kiss *her*, over everybody else — over *me*. Was it her sexy gap-toothed mouth, or the sense that she might not say no to anything at all? But he wasn't like that. And I knew her; I knew that part of her wanted someone else to say no for her, to rescue her from herself — and maybe *that* was what attracted him, smelling that need in her like an animal.)

Halloween, a day I'd always looked forward to, suddenly turned into an ordinary day, even a worse-than-ordinary day, because it held the memory of its specialness. We still decorated the front lawn — the muslin ghosts hanging from the maple branches, the fake spider webs over the holly bushes, the Styrofoam gravestones tucked into the piles of leaves — and my father still carved the pumpkins and put them out with candles in them. We still raided CVS for jumbo bags of mini Snickers and Starbursts and Tootsie Rolls. All those things were the same, but instead of racing through pizza with Cassie and burning my tongue on the melted cheese, then getting hyped and giggly dressing in my room, I sat at the kitchen table with my parents slowly eating pork chops, mashed potatoes, and apple sauce — 'masticating' is the word that comes to mind — interrupted occasionally by the thump of feet on the front steps. I played my mother's role, handing out candy to the little kids whose parents waited in the shadows on the front path. Like my mother always did, I asked in a falsely jolly voice, 'What are *you* meant to be? A burglar! Great costume,' I'd lie. 'You get an extra piece of candy for that.'

The Saghafi kids came as Tweedledum and Tweedledee, and their costumes actually were impressive, made by their mother, involving repurposed baseball shirts and beanie hats and a great deal of wadding that can't just have been cushions because it was too well distributed around their middles. They wore their father's shoes, probably wadded also, so they looked as though they had clown feet. I gave a big thumbs-up to Mrs. Saghafi, who called, 'Not going out this year, Julia?'

I shook my head in a mock dismay that was actually real: 'All good things come to an end, right?' She laughed, and shook her head back.

As the evening wore on, I helped my father with the dishes and my mother took over the candy so I wouldn't have to speak to the bigger kids, most of whom I knew. Inevitably, a posse from my own class turned up, including a girl named Reba from my field hockey team, who saw me lurking and called out, 'Juju, you're not out? Come on, come with us!' I put on an 'I don't care' face and came to the door.

'Naw,' I said, 'I think I'm past it.'

'Don't be so boring!' There was a chorus — not just Reba, but Brent and Joel and Suzanne, dressed as a bee, with translucent wings and an antennae hairband.

'I'm good, guys. Besides, no costume.'

At which point Brent, whose effort consisted of his dad's sports jacket and a porkpie hat, said, 'It doesn't matter. Come without one.'

I laughed, but there were tears right behind. I

waved my dish towel and turned my back. 'Thanks anyway,' I said. 'Have fun. See you in school.'

When she'd closed the door on them, my mother came through and pretended to be looking for *The New Yorker*, but for a moment she put her hand on my shoulder, without speaking; and that was when the tears came, just a couple. Luckily I had my back to her.

'I'm going up to do my homework,' I said. I'd done my homework already, and instead scrolled through Facebook, looking at the photos Cassie had already put up — in real time! — of the Evil Morsel's party, of Mrs. Morsel holding up a tray of decorated cupcakes, and of Peter — handsome Peter, who ought to have been mine — with his left eye and some of his teeth blacked up, wearing an oversized Bruins jersey and wielding a whittled hockey stick dipped in red paint. Delia was dressed as a bunny, a Playboy sort of bunny — how could wholesome-looking Mrs. Vosul have allowed that? — and Cassie, in spite of her white bunny hair, was dressed as a cat, in a cumbersome black velour jumper complete with whiskers, ears, and a tail. I had to smile, because I could see in Cassie's getup the over-vigilant hand of Bev, who would no more have let her daughter out in a Playboy-bunny outfit than gone out that way herself.

'Serious costume!' I commented. 'Sewn by Bev?'

And Cassie texted me to say, 'How well u know my mom. WTF, right? Pickup @9!!'

'School nite?'

'U know it'

'Sorry 4 u'

'Love u Juju,' she wrote back. Enough for me to feel consoled, as though we were suddenly okay, and my mother might be proven right after all.

That wasn't the only time she was sweet to me. There wasn't anything angry or cruel about our drifting, not for her. More like I was an old pair of shoes and she had a couple of fancy new pairs; she didn't think to wear the old ones, but wouldn't have thrown them away. With the Morsel that fall, Cassie moved at speed into a different world, more grown-up than mine, one where she put on different faces for different people. Maybe I made her feel trapped, like she'd outgrown me. But from my side, it was like I knew her too well, I saw her too clearly, when she no longer wanted to be known: she wanted to try out a new role, and didn't want to be reminded that it was fake.

I hoped our family visit at Thanksgiving might bring us back together. In the car with her mother one afternoon, I asked whether Peter would be coming too.

'Peter?' Bev looked at us in the rearview mirror. 'Why would he come?'

'I don't know — I just thought — '

'Cassie, is there anything I should know?'

' 'Course not, Mom.' Cassie used what my mother called 'tone.'

Bev looked again in the rearview, directly at me. 'Cassie's embarrassed, I know, because she wants to be popular. Believe me, I know how it is to be a teenager.' I knew Cassie's mother had never had to worry about being cool. 'Did you not tell her, Cassie?'

'My mother decided,' she began — but Bev, steely but bright, interrupted her.

'No, sweetie. *We* decided. We had a long conversation and *we* decided.'

'*We* decided that I'm too young to have a boyfriend.'

'Not too young to have friends who are boys,' Bev clarified, 'but too young for exclusive relationships.'

'So I told Peter that.'

'So now they're simply friends, not special friends.' Bev wore a tight smile. 'Isn't that right, sweetie?'

Cassie didn't say anything.

'And that's much more appropriate,' Bev concluded. 'It means that they can be friends forever, which they'll both be glad about in time.'

Later, I texted Cassie to ask what had happened.

'Whisker smudge Halloween' she texted back. 'Bad scene omw home' And then, 'Fuck her.' Which wasn't something she would have said easily in earlier times. Cassie and her mother had always been a team, the two of them, and they took care of each other. Cassie made jokes about her mother's outfits, or about how her mother would refuse dessert at our house and eat half a tub of Ben & Jerry's when she got home ('Chunky Monkey for the chunky monkey,'

Cassie would say), but nobody else had ever been allowed to do it. You weren't supposed to laugh too much when Cassie did it, though you were supposed to laugh a little — there was a balance you were expected to find, and I'd long ago figured it out. But the balance had changed. Now there was Peter; now there was the Evil Morsel; now there was Anders Shute. Bev and Cassie weren't on their own anymore; they weren't necessarily a team.

Which became all the more apparent when we stopped by their house on Thanksgiving — my parents and me, although my father had tried at the last minute to stay home with the cousins. My mother had said, 'Rich, you can't possibly bag out. What kind of message does that send? That only the sisterhood can be bothered!' Which both annoyed him and made him laugh.

We'd had twenty-four hours of my father's family by then: my grandfather in headphones on the sofa, conducting an orchestra only he could hear, while the eight-year-old twins, Brad and Joe, Mike and Eileen's youngest, chased each other noisily around him. My grandmother spent a great deal of time in the kitchen, 'helping.' She added seasonings to my mother's sauces; she rearranged the flower arrangements; she polished the special-occasion silverware as if my mother hadn't spent the previous Sunday doing it. Nana Robinson was never still or quiet. She loved to talk, she loved to laugh; she loved a party and a crowd.

'If only she loved to listen,' my mother would whisper, only then to apologize. We adored

Nana; it was just difficult having her as a houseguest. Grandpa too adored her, but he found it difficult sometimes having her as a wife — hence the headphones: expensive Bose noise-cancelling ones that removed him, immediately and entirely, to an encompassing aural universe of his own choosing. He was a lover of Satie and Debussy, of limpid, private music; Nana was more like Wagner.

As for Mike and Eileen and their four children: the twins essentially counted as a single, lunatic kid. Jake, the eldest, was like Grandpa in his retreat. Lanky, seventeen, with big glasses that enlarged his dark eyes and a rash of little red spots on his porcelain-white forehead, he wasn't doomed to be a gamer; he was one by choice. He could actually have been — and would soon thereafter become — fairly handsome. He didn't have a speech impediment or halitosis. His dark hair was curly, his full-lipped mouth kind of sexy. But that fall he spent most of their visit in the attic guest room, plugged into an alternative game world — 'Like a cockroach,' his mother joked. 'Only comes out when the lights are off.'

Their sister, Una, was closest to me in age — ten that fall, in fifth grade. She'd always admired me; imitation is the highest form of flattery, as my mother says. When I loved Harry Potter, she copied me. When I wore Doc Martens, she wanted a pair. When I got bangs in the fifth grade, we sent the cousins my school photo, and the next time we saw her, she had bangs that brushed the top of her glasses. But that year, the distance between fifth grade and seventh grade seemed unbridgeably huge, and looking at her bright eyes behind their thick glasses and at the pink baubles in her hair, at her flat little Gumby body that could still easily perform backflips and cartwheels, that had no lumps or odorous emanations or secretions to mask — it was like looking back across a rough channel to a shore upon which you'd never again set foot. So I'd been mostly avoiding Una, and her eager conversation about books or shows or movies or pop stars. I wanted to say to her, *Can't you see I'm contaminated? Can't you see the grown-up dirt all over me?*

My mother was annoyed with me throughout their visit — ostensibly because I wasn't being a good enough hostess to the cousins, but really because she found it overwhelming to have so many members of my father's family staying; but they were all so good-natured that she couldn't show it, or even allow that she was mildly irritable. The cousins were there on my father's account, and she wanted *very much* to be a good enough person not to be annoyed, because he himself was that sort of good person, and put up with my mother's family without ever, apparently, losing his temper. So I was the only person she could lash out at in good conscience. She knew it, and I knew it, and I tried not to take her outbursts to heart.

The three of us went over to the Burneses' in my mother's car around six p.m. — 'I think you'd better drive, honey,' my father said — and left the cousins to watch *Night at the Museum*

2, the only film they could agree on.

The Burnes house was lit up like a stage set, all the windows bright, and the Aucoins' dogs barked when we pulled up. You could smell their fire in the chill night air, and from the houses on either side you could hear vague partyish noises and see moving shadows behind the blinds. In spite of all the lights at the Burneses', it was quiet and still. When we rang the doorbell, Cassie opened at once as if she'd been standing there, waiting. She had her phone in her hand and quickly stuffed it into her pocket.

Cassie acted with my parents as though everything was normal — best behavior, super polite — and in the flurry got by with a quick 'Hey, Juju' to me. She led us into the living room — about three steps to our left — where Bev, in royal-blue chiffon, looking like an opera singer, stood imposingly next to Dr. Anders Shute. I knew straightaway who he was.

Bev introduced us and we sat, as if on cue. They'd pulled in a dining chair ahead of time, to have exactly the right number of seats for the six of us. On the glass coffee table sat a harvest arrangement from the florist in Royston — I'd seen them in the window all week — involving autumn leaves and a warty mini-gourd and an elaborate bow of sparkly russet ribbon. I wondered whether Bev had bought it or Anders Shute had given it as a gift. The gourd resembled an ugly man's face, and I thought that in a different moment, Cassie and I would have laughed about that.

'You look so familiar . . . ' My mother actually

clapped her hands. 'Of course! Dr. Shute! You patched up poor Cassie at the hospital this summer.'

'That's right,' he said with a thin sliver of a smile, his voice soft. 'We patched her up.'

'The importance of being patient,' my mother went on. 'Don't be the *im*-patient! Such a good line. Of course.'

He dipped his head, still slightly smiling.

'So is that how you guys met?' My father leaned forward in the La-Z-Boy and his flannel trousers rustled on the leatherette. 'Clue me in.'

'No, no.' Bev waved her elegant little hands — she'd painted her nails to match her dress, only a more silvery sort of blue — 'We met in church.'

'So you didn't know — ' My mother looked from one to the other.

'Oh, we figured it out pretty quick. Even before Cassie came into the room. Talk about coincidences, right?'

Anders Shute nodded some more. Still the little smile. He looked as though his jacket, shirt, and tie had all been clipped on, the way you clip clothes on paper dolls, and they're always a little askew. Everything hung a bit wrong: the collar, the sleeves. Maybe he was just too skinny.

'Yeah, crazy, right?' Cassie said. 'Like, what are the odds?'

'You have to believe the Lord has a plan for us,' Bev said. 'Isn't it amazing?' She pushed herself up from the sofa in one swift movement. 'Now, who-all is ready for a little pie?'

My parents and I made eager noises.

'I've laid everything out on the dining table, so let's all go help ourselves; and then we can sit back down and get to know one another.' She paused in the doorway, flushed and almost pretty for a second. 'I'm so pleased that we're getting together. I've been looking forward to this.'

It occurred to me that she was proud not only to have a date — Bev had never had a boyfriend after Clarke, not in all Cassie's life; she hadn't wanted to — but also that she was proud to show Dr. Shute that she was friends with my father, the dentist; and that she was proud to show my parents that her beau, worth waiting so long for, was a doctor, which on some invisible scale trumped 'dentist' anytime. When Bev said she was so pleased, she really meant it. She had planned for that moment, had probably imagined it a dozen times.

I was waiting for Cassie to signal to me that we could escape upstairs to her room. I couldn't believe that she wouldn't, but as we sat pinkening in the too-hot living room, with the fire crackling and the grown-ups droning ('Then seven years in Bangor,' Dr. Shute was saying, 'at the hospital there . . . ') and the pecan pie so sweet — sweeter than Nana's, if that was possible — that it made my back right molar ache and made me aware of a new cavity . . . as this went on and on, I thought with a sudden lurch that maybe I'd been fantasizing, that things between us were even worse than I'd imagined and that the punishment for my newly demoted status was to stay trapped on the puffy chintz for the entire visit. I worried that Cassie would rather suffer the boring adults than hang out with me alone.

But eventually, in a voice so naturally kind that only I could tell she was acting, Cassie offered to make more coffee for everyone, and suggested that I come with her. In the kitchen, things felt strange for a moment, but our familiarity, so deep in our bones, won out; and she hadn't finished scooping the Starbucks Colombian Dark Roast into the Coffeemaster before I said, 'What the fuck, Cassie? How did this happen? Your mom's been shot by Shute! Why didn't you say?'

'It's not a fricking joke, Juju.'

'But how long?'

'He first came home a few weeks ago. Like a horrible Halloween ghost, the morning after. Right after we had the big blow-out about Peter.'

'Was that bad?'

She snorted, fiddling with the water tap and the coffee pot. ''Was that bad?' It was fucking insane. My mother pulled me up the stairs by my hair. I'm surprised there isn't a hole in my scalp.'

'For real?'

'For real.' And then: 'All we did was make out. For Christ's sake, it was a party. Delia's mom and dad were in the next room. But Bev went psycho. Cue the horror music.'

'Shit,' I said.

'She'd been seeing him' — she nodded toward the living room — 'for, like, a month before she brought him home. The first time I saw them talking at the church group was the day after Columbus Day.' She didn't hesitate over the date; she had it firmly recorded. Columbus Day weekend, I'd gone with my parents to New York City, where we'd all stayed in one hotel room and my mother had got tickets to *Wicked*. Anders Shute — we'd met him together, practically sisters in the ER, hardly four months before.

'What's he like?'

'Exactly like he seems.'

'Thin?' Hoping for a laugh.

'He wasn't a church guy. He'd never been to our church even once, and then he shows up, like that, at Bible study. What's that about?'

'Did someone bring him along?' At our house, we mocked Bev's Bible study group as an alternative dating site for the socially impaired. But I wouldn't ever before have shared that with Cassie. 'You know, was he with a friend of his?'

'He didn't know a soul. He made a point of it. He said he read about the meeting on the bulletin board at the Market Basket. Do you believe that?'

'Lonely guy.'

'Here's what I believe,' she said. 'I believe he was looking for us — for me. I believe he found out about the youth group because of our photo album online. And then he figured out about the Bible study, and Mom, and then he came there. He doesn't even live in Royston, for fuck's sake. He lives in *Haverhill*, and he works in *Haverhill*.'

'That doesn't seem too likely, does it?'

'Doesn't it?'

'Wouldn't there be easier ways to find you

than pretending in some long-term way to be a practicing Christian?'

'There might be easier ways, but it's a pretty certain way to my mom's heart. She's totally gone on him. It's surreal.'

I thought a minute. 'Why do you think he was looking for you? Is he, like, creepy or scary around you? Does he say stuff? Or — '

'No.' She leaned in and whispered, and I was gratefully aware of his even voice from the other room: he was still holding forth about the differences in the medical profession between Maine and Massachusetts. 'It's the opposite. He doesn't look at me. He doesn't speak to me. He doesn't stay in a room with me if she walks out of it. He'll make up some reason to leave.'

'That sounds like a good thing, no? You wouldn't want to have to talk to him on your own.'

'God, no. But it's weird. Admit it, it's really weird.'

'But he *is* weird. It's the most obvious thing about him. Maybe he's embarrassed.'

'Embarrassed?'

'When he realized you were Bev's daughter — maybe that somehow makes it strange, that he'd already met you, but not her.'

Cassie snorted.

'Or maybe he's embarrassed' — I knew that here I was on thin ice — 'that being so slight himself, he likes a larger lady?'

Cassie snapped a dish towel at me, but I could see the thought was a relief — that his hidden perversion might just be an attraction to plumpness. She even smiled. 'That is *not* kind to my mom,' she said. And then, 'She hasn't deserved my kindness much lately.'

'Tell me about the Peter thing, then.'

'Let me take this coffee in, and then we'll go upstairs.'

⋆ ⋆ ⋆

Later, in the car on the way home, my mother was furious with me. 'You girls were so rude,' she hissed. My father sighed. 'I was ashamed of you both. Cassie — well, it's none of my business, but really, Julia, you're old enough to know better.'

'Come on, Carole,' my father said, emasculated in the passenger seat. 'You're being a bit harsh, don't you think? They're kids.'

'They laughed at him, Rich! Obviously too. So rude.'

'I don't even know what you're talking about.'

'When you came in with the coffee and stood in the doorway and rolled your eyes while he was speaking — '

'*He* didn't see,' I said, 'and Bev had her back to us.'

'That's not the point, Julia, and you know it.'

'He did go on a bit,' my father said. 'Nothing against the guy, but he seems a little . . . almost — '

'He's, like, autistic or something, right?'

Normally, my mother would have laughed. She would have been on my side. 'So you're a neurologist or a psychiatrist now? You're diagnosing people at age twelve? Where do you get off?'

'But Mom — '

'And if he *were* on the spectrum, would that be something to titter about? If he had one leg, or if he was deaf, would you make fun of him?'

'Of course not — but Mom — '

'It seems to me profoundly lacking in charity, as well as good manners. I don't like to think that's how we've raised you. Shame on you.'

'Carole, that's a bit much.' My father put his hand on her arm, but she had her hand on the steering wheel and jerked it as she knocked him away. The car swerved on the median. Luckily there was no other traffic. 'Hey babe, it's not worth an accident!' My father's voice was quiet, but I could tell he was shocked. 'What are you so worked up about?'

'I don't know.' My mother's voice was suddenly quiet too, as if she'd scared herself. 'I don't know.'

We were silent for a minute. Then I apologized. 'We didn't mean to behave badly,' I said. 'We just wanted to go upstairs, you know?'

My mother took a deep breath. 'I know, sweetie. I overreacted.' And a minute later: 'There was something so not-right about it all.'

'Doesn't mean it was Julia's fault. Or even Cassie's.' My dad fiddled with the vents. 'He's an odd duck, Shute.'

'Bev's not exactly run-of-the-mill herself,' my mother conceded. 'I'm glad for her. She's been alone a long time.'

'No, she hasn't,' I said. 'She has Cassie.'

'You know that's not what I meant.'

'You mean, better a date with Anders Shute from Maine than another secret tryst with her friends Ben & Jerry from Vermont?'

'Rich!' She shook her head, but she wasn't really angry anymore. 'Shame on *you*. Now I see where our daughter gets it from.'

We pulled into our driveway and could see everyone through the living-room window, dimly but arrestingly lit. Grandpa was slumped, asleep on the sofa, with Una rapt beside him, knees to her chest, in her candy-colored onesie pajamas, her glasses reflecting the TV's light. Grandma knitted busily while Jake sprawled on the floor with his phone, eyes on the little screen rather than the big one. Mike and Eileen and the twins weren't in the picture — presumably the twins were in bed — but even without them the scene looked so cozy and normal. So safe, was what I thought.

⋆ ⋆ ⋆

It's hard to grasp all the different things that are going on at one time, or that went on at one time. That fall in art class, I learned about the Spanish painter Goya — our art teacher was obsessed with him — and I ended up writing a paper about his life. Only much later, when we learned about the French Revolution in world history, did I realize Goya was getting going as a court painter in Madrid at the same time as Marie Antoinette was having her head chopped off. You'd never think it. Spain and France are right next to each other, but it was as if he were on a different planet — in the same way that he was in seventh-grade art class for me, and the French Revolution was in ninth-grade history, and who was going to make the connection?

That's sort of what happened with Cassie and me. I guess I was Goya, just doing my thing, and she was the French Revolution.

* * *

After Thanksgiving, Mr. Cartwright, who taught honors English, took me aside and asked if I'd like to join the speech team. It was prestigious: our middle school had been best or second-best in the state for six years running, winning awards and even competing in Washington, DC. It didn't occur to me not to do it. I was launched into a schedule of after-school practices and tournaments and new people, and it wasn't so easy to carpool with the Burneses. Often, my mother picked me up after dark, and I'd come out of school to see our blue Subaru wagon lonely in a corner of the lot with its headlights off, identifiable because my mother had the interior light on, and her reading glasses, and was lost in an issue of *Harper's* or *The New Yorker*. The other parents kept the headlights on and the interior light off, listening to the radio maybe.

Jodie and Jensen were my new speech team friends. They came from Georgetown, sister and brother, a year apart, sandy, wiry, and strong on the team. Jensen, the elder, in eighth grade, did political speeches mostly, and the debate side of speech; whereas Jodie, who was in my English class, preferred inspirational stuff or monologues from plays, and was really an actress. In class, she was quiet, almost mousy, which was why I hadn't noticed her earlier; but onstage she was transformed. Her version of the 'I Have a Dream' speech made me cry.

Sometimes at the weekends when there wasn't a tournament, Jodie and I would get together and practice our pieces, or do some homework, or hang out, checking out possible monologues on YouTube. We gossiped about our crushes — film and music stars, mostly, but sometimes guys on speech teams from other schools, glimpsed, competed against, romanticized. Sometimes with Jodie — and occasionally with Jodie and Jensen together — I'd find myself doing something I thought of distinctly as Cassie's and mine, like baking banana bread, or browsing the stuffed animal collection at Bell's. I'd catch my breath: did she still sleep with Hubert the pig? Did the Evil Morsel like to bake? But mostly, I was okay with seeing her sometimes at lunch — on Wednesdays, our lunch periods were the same, and Delia had a class, so Cassie and I would sit together then, especially after she broke up with Peter.

And on the Fridays when I didn't have speech team, we'd get picked up together, usually by my mother. Cassie always said she had to get home, even though Bev wouldn't be there for hours yet. We'd drop her at her house, a little girl on the doorstep of the little white house with the

Encroaching Forest looming behind. It made me nervous — like something out of a scary movie, especially in winter when night came in fast. But Cassie didn't seem bothered. When I asked if she got scared, ever, in that house alone, she raised a contemptuous eyebrow.

'We're old enough to babysit, right? So I think I can babysit myself, don't you?'

I wanted to point out that when you babysat, there was another person in the house with you, if only a little person who'd be no help in a crisis. But I knew she'd mock me. If she wasn't scared — didn't she watch *CSI* too? Or *Criminal Minds*? — then why would I make her scared? That would have been cruel.

But I did wonder what she *did*, on those afternoons — not just Fridays either, because on the days I had speech team, somebody else's mother or father dropped her at her door. It seemed like a lot of time to be alone. When I was by myself — and I loved being in my room on my own, reading on my bed or listening to music and staring at the glow-in-the-dark stars that my father had stuck on the ceiling when I was small — I could hear my mother moving around the house, the creaky boards upstairs or the faint murmur of the radio from the kitchen, and then I could smell dinner: the onions in the pan, or the whiff of meat cooking or the delicious pastry scent of a baking tart. Even when I was alone, I liked to know that I wasn't really entirely alone; but that wasn't how it was for Cassie.

All those years we'd been friends, since

forever, we'd used the same words and perhaps meant different things — sometimes slightly different, but other times radically dissimilar; and we'd never known it. As if I'd been holding an apple and thinking it was a tennis ball, all this time. Like 'home': to me, it meant our creaky old house with noisy forced-air heating and rattly windows, made small and familiar by the endless piles of magazines and folded laundry that my mother left around, by the classical music or the radio voices in the background, by the comings and goings of friends and relations, and the knowledge that even when my father was 'at work,' I could open my window and throw a ball (or an apple), and practically hit him. Almost every day, my parents hugged me; and when I read in bed at night, one of them almost always came to give me a kiss before I turned out the light, a leftover from my early childhood of which I was still fond. 'Home' was that feeling of falling asleep to the distant muffle of your parents' conversation, a sound rising through the floorboards almost as a reverberation not just in your ears but in your body. It was a particular set of familiar smells — the orange-flower soap in the downstairs bathroom, or the tinge of old fire smoke in the living room even in summertime, when it rained — and patches of warm air near the vents, followed by a chill near the windows. It was the knowledge that someone was always nearby. And if not, then the Saghafis were right next door, and the whole of town, a constant little burble, right down the road. The Rite Aid, after all, stayed open till midnight. If I needed to run screaming into the street, someone would hear me.

* * *

Sometimes I felt that growing up and being a girl was about learning to be afraid. Not paranoid, exactly, but always alert and aware, like checking out the exits in the movie theater or the fire escape in a hotel. You came to know, in a way you hadn't as a kid, that the body you inhabited was vulnerable, imperfectly fortified. On TV, in the papers, in books and movies, it isn't ever men being raped or kidnapped or bludgeoned or dismembered or burned with acid. But in stories and crime shows and TV series and movies and in life too, it's going on all the time, all around you. So you learn, in your mind, that your body needs to be protected. It's both precious and totally dispensable, depending on whom you encounter. You don't want to end up at a party not knowing how to get home. You don't want to end up walking down a street — especially a quiet street — by yourself at night. You don't want to open your door to a strange man at all, really, ever, if you're alone, even if he's wearing a uniform. Because his uniform could be a disguise. It happens. I've seen it on TV.

You start to grow up and you learn from all the stories around you what the world is like, and you start to lose freedoms. Not because anybody actually tells you that you've lost them, but because you know you need to take care. Without a friend beside you, no biking on the

Audubon Trail, no swimming at the quarry, no hiking in the woods. Beware darkness, isolation, the outdoors, unlocked windows, men you don't know. And then you realize too that even men you know, or thought you knew, might not be okay.

A math teacher that fall at a high school in nearby New Hampshire was caught in an FBI sting with thousands of kiddie-porn images on his computer — pictures of little girls kept in cages, someone said. A rabbi in Boston was caught spying on the women of his congregation in their ritual baths. The guy who owned the diner we'd sometimes gone to on our way back from the beach, less than half an hour from our house, was accused of sexually harassing his waitresses and forcing one — or was it three? Or five? They kept coming out of the woodwork; it had gone on for years, apparently — to have sex with him. So when I remembered the harried woman in tight mom jeans who'd served us the last time — memorable for a strawberry birthmark the size of a gumball on her right cheek, and for the fact that, with her heavily outlined china-blue eyes, she was otherwise notably pretty, or had been, until life had ground her down and worn her out prematurely, furrowing her skin — I remembered her and wondered if she was one of them, if she'd been forced onto her knees in the pantry after hours, or whether the birthmark had spared her, like what Cassie had told me about the sign from God at Passover, whether her flaw had proven her blessed protection.

You get to middle school, and you think about these things. The world opens up; history stretches behind you, and the future stretches before you, and you're suddenly aware of the wild, unknowable interior lives of everyone around you, the realization that each and every person lives in an unspoken world as full and strange as your own, and that you can't ever hope entirely to know anything, not even yourself.

But just as the world is opening up, it's closing too, and things reveal their previously unimagined shapes. Without it being said, I was treated as a kid with a bright future and Cassie, well, she wasn't necessarily *not* going to have one, but her path would be different from mine. Without anybody saying so outright, I was being told that my path was the more valuable. I got that from my parents, and from Mr. Cartwright when he chose me for speech team, and from my teachers when they patted me on the back and gave me good grades, and from my grandmother, who, when she asked me about Cassie at Thanksgiving and I told her we'd been drifting apart, caressed my cheek with her shiny hand that smelled of rosewater and said, 'It's hard growing up, because each of us must follow our own star' — which was, of itself, pretty neutral, but then she added, 'And some of us have brighter stars to follow than others, I'm afraid.'

And if we were growing up, and growing up differently now, and if there was some faintly ominous sense about the adolescence and adulthood that lay before us — as if there'd inevitably be a cull along the way, and drugs, or violence, or car crashes or general misfortune, or, for the girls, the folly of careless sex or the evils of predatory men who lurked, unidentifiable as guerilla fighters, among us — then the unspoken cry that echoed from all sides was 'Save yourself!' because it was clear that it was the only thing you could hope to do, and even that might be impossible.

You couldn't possibly try to save someone else first. Like the safety demonstration on the airplane, when they tell you to put on your own oxygen mask first. That's what matters. You can't help anyone if you don't help yourself.

Cassie wasn't herself thinking about any of these things, as far as I know. Not then or later. It was a preoccupying riff in my own head. My mother made me stop watching crime programs on TV, and when the girl in New Hampshire, a couple of years older than Cassie and me, vanished on her way home from school, my mother stopped leaving the local paper around and turned off the news if the story came on. Around the same time, there was the young woman at college in Portland whose body was never found: they figured out that a guy she knew from her job had invited her home to hang out with him and his girlfriend, and then they'd killed her and thrown her body into the ocean. You had to wonder why they'd done it. Just because they could? And you had to wonder about that girlfriend. What was going on in *her* head? What kind of person was she?

'The depravity!' my mother ranted. 'It's a

self-perpetuating cycle in a sick society.' And then: 'As a feminist, I've got to find a way for us to address this.'

'Us?'

'You and me.'

'What are you talking about?'

'I wish this wasn't the world,' she said. 'Part of me wants to protect you from hearing it . . . but this *is* the world.' She shrugged. 'So we have to find some way to address it.'

Whether because of the facts, or the culture, or my mother's anger about it, or simply my cowardly temperament, the only result was that I was scared, some type of low-level scared all the time — in the back of my mind, but always there.

Cassie wasn't, or she wasn't letting on. If I was melting into a state of near-constant anxiety, my body creating palpitations and tremors out of innocuous sounds, then Cassie was hardening, small, tight, unsparing, even her laugh turned brittle, and her little girl's body seemed at once unfinished and withering on the vine. She told me some stuff when we were together, but always as if it were a joke, a black joke. I figured it was how she got by.

First, Anders Shute spent more and more time at their house. Thank God for the hospital, she said, because sometimes he'd stay away several days at a stretch, on account of his rotation schedule. But then, in the New Year . . . It was after she'd really broken up with Peter Oundle — not just pretended to, for her mother's sake. I only understood much later, from him, and to my profound surprise, that their breakup was over a big argument they'd had where he'd told her she needed to confront Bev and tell her it couldn't work with Anders Shute, that his presence made Cassie miserable; and Cassie told Peter to mind his own fucking business, that she'd seen her mom sad and lonely all her life — all Cassie's life, that is — and that Bev had made a thousand sacrifices for Cassie over the years, hadn't thought of being loved by a man on account of Cassie, and had given up hope of it; and that she, Cassie, wasn't going to be the reason her mother ended up unhappy all over again.

It was the opposite of what I would've expected, but it made sense too. Cassie and Bev were like tree trunks grown together. She depended on her mother, and vice versa, and she couldn't possibly be happy if she felt responsible for her mother's unhappiness. But what about her own?

Anyway, Cassie broke up with Peter, saying that he wanted too much from her. He said he got it, sort of: it wasn't like she liked someone else. It was about her and Bev, really: her mom believed that Cassie and Peter had broken up at Halloween. It's tiring to lie and to pretend your boyfriend isn't someone special, when not only your mother but also this other random guy is watching your every move.

Peter was badly hurt — he told me so, and even months later he would have got back together with her in a minute, if she'd wanted. 'I've liked her for ages,' he confided. 'Remember last summer, when you guys were walking past our basketball game, and Beckett yelled something rude? I knew you'd laugh it off, but I could tell she was pissed. And I came after you guys because I wanted her to know it wasn't me.'

'You wanted her to like you.'

'Yeah.'

He *felt* a lot — he feels a lot — Peter, even though he didn't want people to see it. He wanted to be cool, and emotion wasn't; but he couldn't help feeling. That all seemed so clear to me — it was part of what I'd always loved about him. You could say, in a way, that I loved how much he loved Cassie: I just wished it were me instead. And she? I don't think she knew it for love, not then. She wasn't earnest in that same way. She was, somehow, a little cold inside — actually cool. It was the right word. It was part of what both Peter and I loved about her.

As for Cassie's other friendships, needless to say, Bev didn't like the Evil Morsel any more than I did, though I'd like to think that at least some of her reasons were different. But it meant Cassie didn't talk much about school at home, or vice versa. She segregated these two sections of her life, lived two lives. She kept lipstick and eyeliner and jeans with holes in them in her locker along with makeup-remover pads, and she took to dressing a second time before the first bell and a third time after the last one. From what little Cassie conveyed to me, Delia thought it was funny. I might have found it funny too if we'd still been close, but when I told Jodie, she rolled her pristine, un-made-up hazel eyes and whispered, 'Doesn't that just strike you as so *sad*? I mean, almost pathetic? Like, why doesn't she feel okay being who she is, instead of putting on a disguise, like a costume, every morning?'

'What if she feels like the person she is at home is the one in disguise, though? And like she's not allowed to be her real self when she's there?'

Jodie shook her head. 'That's just sad, you know?'

In the New Year, maybe late February or so — after Valentine's Day, and maybe it was even decided then, in the course of an evening Bev and Anders Shute spent canoodling over lo mein and a tiki candle at the Lotus Garden on Route 29, while Cassie sat at home with Electra on her lap, watching reruns of *Friends* and texting with Delia — Dr. Anders Shute formally moved into the picturesque white Cape with its skirt of fence.

Cassie said that they'd sat her down and explained that they were married in the eyes of God. They'd prayed about it together, Bev and Anders Shute told her — they sat on the sofa holding hands while they talked, Cassie said, and they finished each other's sentences — and God had blessed them as man and wife. If they weren't yet married in a courthouse, Anders Shute said, it was only because of her, because of Cassie: they didn't want to complicate things legally until Cassie was comfortable. This, Anders Shute made clear, was Bev's wish. But they would henceforth be a Family — Cassie said they both kept saying the word as if it had a capital letter — and Anders Shute said she must think of him as her Father (again, a capital letter); and that sentence, Cassie said, Bev made no move to finish for him. But when he said it, Cassie saw that Bev couldn't look at her, but looked instead down at her lap. 'Because she knew,' Cassie said, 'that it was fat fucking chance. Like anyone but my real dad could ever, ever be my father.'

Dr. Anders Shute abandoned his apartment in Haverhill, put his furniture in storage (with the exception of a few inexplicable artifacts: a signed Red Sox baseball in a satin-lined box; a garish and not-small painting of a sunset in Maine involving boulders, seascape, and great swathes of pink and purple, all in an ornate gilded frame; and a large orange-and-yellow blown-glass display bowl that looked so much like a wedding gift that you wanted to ask him whether he had, in fact, been married) and arrived, according to Cassie, on a Sunday afternoon, with three large suitcases and a box of books, in his silver-green Honda Civic that matched Bev's crimson one, only it was a newer model. In bulk, his clothes, Cassie said, smelled like the health-food store, that particular vitamin stink that seeps from the pill bottles and makes you want to gag. She was also perturbed to find that he — like she herself — used Clairol Herbal Essences shampoo *and* conditioner on his lank locks, and blue Listerine mouthwash for his gums.

'Just the idea of him in our bathroom grosses me out,' she told me one early spring lunchtime in the cafeteria. Under the fluorescent light, her eyes were red-rimmed and her nostrils too — she had a more powerful white-rabbit aspect than usual.

'But do you still think he's so . . . '

'Of course.' She turned to her french fries, swiping a couple at a time through their glob of ketchup. 'But mostly, an asshole.'

'Asshole. Oh no. How so?'

'You know how he'd never been to church, I think, before joining Mom's Bible study class? Well, it's like he's now the most Christian of all.' She shook her head. 'Is he trying to impress Mom? Does he really believe this shit? Or is it some calculated way to control us — to control me?'

'Like how?'

'Like, there's the clothes and makeup thing — '

I looked at her black concert T-shirt and her torn jeans, her raccoon eyes and purple lipstick. 'You seem to be dodging that bullet pretty well so far.'

'So far, yeah, but you have no idea. They check my closet. They 'confiscated' three skirts for being 'too short.' He told her my party heels were too high. I had to take down some of my posters — like the *Supernatural* one, because he said it wasn't 'appropriate,' because there are demons on the show.'

'Or is it because the actors are too hot?'

'Maybe that too. But suddenly they want to know every YouTube video I watch, every website I visit, every book I read, every song I listen to . . . '

'And that's him? Or your mom too?'

'It's both of them. But it's coming from him.'

'How do you know?'

'I just know.'

I believed her. You didn't have to be a shrink to see he could get Bev to do almost anything he wanted. 'What about the other thing?'

'What other thing?'

'Well, you thought . . . you said before, at Thanksgiving, that maybe he — ' If she didn't remember what she'd said, I shouldn't remind her. It was good if she'd forgotten; it meant it wasn't true.

'You mean that I thought he'd gone looking for me. That he'd found my mom because he wanted to get to me. That's what you mean, right?'

I nodded. I didn't understand why I felt embarrassed, but I did.

'Look,' she said, and because I knew her as well as I knew myself, I could tell she was both serious and sort of acting at the same time; she was 'acting serious,' as if she were in an episode of *Supernatural* or something like it, a teen psychodrama that both was and wasn't like life. 'Look, I don't exactly know what he's trying to do. But he looks at me sometimes — I catch him looking at me through those little eyes — and the hairs on the back of my neck stand up.'

'But does he — '

'He doesn't *do* anything. He doesn't *say* anything. Nothing I could point to and get him in trouble for. Nothing you'd know was wrong. But he's just *off*, right? He's started coming out with quotations from the Bible — 'from scripture,' he calls it — and it always seems like he's boning up, like he's been memorizing this shit for homework — '

'Like what kind of stuff?'

'You know, 'The works of the flesh are manifest, which are these: adultery, fornication, uncleanness, lasciviousness . . . ' or 'Whoever conceals their sins does not prosper, but the one who confesses and renounces them finds mercy' — crazy, bullying stuff.'

'And your mom?'

'My mom is like . . . it's like he's literally sent by God. Like she never thought she could be so lucky.' Cassie looked down at the table and for a second there was no pretense, no mask on her face, and her expression was baffled and sad. She looked like the little kid she had been. 'I don't want to be the one to ruin it for her, you know? I can't do that.'

I'd heard this already from Peter. But her despair felt real, as if it had a color and filled the air. It was ochre. Ochre and acrid.

'What can I do, Cass? What can I do to help?'

She switched back to her masked self, with a sharp bark of laughter. Mirthless. 'Delia says I can come live at her place — how do you think that'll go down?'

'Badly.' I was trying to pull her back to me, to get the real girl to return. 'But your mom might not say no to me, to my mom, if you wanted to come live at our place for a while. I can easily ask — '

'That's so sweet of you, Juju. You've always

been the sweetest. But you know I couldn't live at your house. That would never work.'

'Why not? We've got lots of room, and your mom knows us so well — '

'Trust me' — and she even put her hand on my forearm, as if the director of the TV episode had suggested the gesture, that it would demonstrate the right combination of condescension and fakery — 'it just isn't a good idea.'

My new friends, people like Jodie and Jensen, couldn't fathom my loyalty to Cassie. There was some leeway when you'd been friends since nursery school. We all made exceptions in our judgment for things like that. But Cassie's tone when she said I couldn't help her — I saw, suddenly, that while I'd felt our friendship, though in a bumpy stretch, was still the most precious, she thought she could laugh at me to my face. If I'd been going around with my mother's words in my head ('Wait and it will change!' . . . 'Things look different depending on where you stand!'), she'd been going around with a distinct hierarchy in hers, in which she was Regina George from *Mean Girls* and I was Janis. Frankly, if she wanted to play that game, I could list a dozen ways in which I was her superior, from my grades to my parents' house to my boobs to my morals. I wasn't proud of my internal rant — I knew better than to speak these ugly thoughts aloud, even to my mother, but I had them. I wasn't just hurt but I hated her a little too.

I discovered I could hate her a bit, and because I didn't tell her so, because our friendship went along on this reduced, part-time scale that didn't allow for arguments, there was no noticeable change in our relationship. She didn't know my feelings had changed — and I assumed she couldn't tell. I could also add to my list of superiorities the fact that I was more observant and sensitive than she, that I could tell when she was being fake but the reverse wasn't apparently true.

That spring, I had a busy exterior life, between school and speech team; but I had a busy interior life too, listening to Cassie's intimacies as if I were still her loving friend, while feeling like a spy, gathering data for a professional report.

That wasn't why I became friends with Peter. He'd sought me out that winter after things between him and Cassie ended. We didn't hang out at school — he was a jock, a track star, hot even when his hair was dark with sweat, and into math and science. But he called me one night in January, and invited me to meet up at the diner in Royston to talk about Cassie, because he said he was worried about her. That was when he told me about their breakup, how it had been her choice, but he secretly hoped they could work things out.

After that, we'd speak often on the phone, maybe even a few times a week, a strange friendship, rarely face-to-face in the beginning. There wasn't, in our middle school lives, another way for us to spend time together. And while at first we talked mostly about Cassie — how she didn't seem really to know herself, and how

Delia had too much influence over her, and how she was turning, heliotropically, to the dark sun of the party crowd in a way that dismayed Peter, who so passionately wanted to be her savior — over time we talked about other things too: the pressures he felt from his parents (his dad was an engineer at Henkel and his mom had a general law practice in Newburyport, 'nothing fancy,' he said, but for her to be a lawyer was fancy enough, and put him in the subset of kids at school in which I also found myself, of whom things were expected), or the school gossip (what parties there'd been, although he went to them and mostly I didn't, and what funny or shocking or predictable things people had done, or how drunk or high they'd been), or funny observations about teachers or kids at school. He had a sense of humor and noticed things — that Monsieur Favreau, the Canadian French teacher who coached hockey too, sounded like a quacking duck when he made announcements on the PA; or that when nobody took down the popped balloons in the gym after the winter dance, their rubber corpses dangled like brightly colored condoms for a week; or that the smell in the cafeteria on chili days was oddly like the whiff he got when bagging the family Labrador's steaming turds. He made me laugh; I made him laugh; and yes, Cassie was between us, our friendship's reason for being, but she came to seem less the entire point of it as winter turned to spring.

She wasn't coming back to him either. That became clear. She acted out at parties that winter, drinking and flirting and slipping into dark corners with other guys. That's what Peter told me; but when I asked her about it — 'be careful,' I warned, nannyish but sincere — she told me that she knew what she was doing, that she never had more than couple of drinks. ('Think about it, Juju,' she said. 'My mom picks me up from every single party. If I was blitzed don't you think she'd know right away? She's a *nurse*, for fuck's sake.') She assured me she didn't get high; she said she'd never done more than make out with guys, though she did admit that there were several of them, and they were always in eighth grade and sometimes even in ninth.

I wanted to believe her; but Peter told me other things, and he had no reason to make them up. Looking back, I wonder if she told me what she wanted to be the truth; but I still can't square it all with Bev and Anders Shute, who would have dressed her as a Mennonite if they'd been able but who never stopped her going to parties in the first place. Did they only pretend to pay attention, when really they were too wrapped up in each other? Or did Bev have mixed motives — my mother always says that 'people are contradictory' — and even while Bev ramped up her own religious devotion, she secretly, even unconsciously, loved that Cassie was a cool kid, behaving in ways Bev would only have dreamed of, accepted by people who, in Bev's day, would have shunned her?

Or was Cassie just turning into a very good liar, with her sweet little-girl face, those big eyes, and that pure, pristine near-white hair dazzling the grown-ups into believing what she wanted them to? When she told *me* that she was fine, that she was in control, that she knew her limits, I believed her. Sitting across from her in the cafeteria, with its prison lights and its bad smells, *I believed her*. Only later, talking to Peter, I wondered, and doubted, and frankly disbelieved.

I defended her though. People started to say things, to assume things, to repeat them. Jouncing along on the bus on the way to a speech tournament, when the first cherry blossoms were out like girls in prom dresses, and the rain on the highway made a slick slurping sound beneath the tires, Jodie asked me if it was true that Cassie had been in the boys' locker room after school, doing things.

'Doing what things?'

'You know. Things. A bunch of guys from the boys' lacrosse team were there, and so was Cassie. Those kind of things.'

'That's crap, Jodie.' My hands trembled in my lap. 'I can't believe you'd even repeat that kind of garbage. What if it was you?'

'It would never be me.'

'You don't know that. People have it in for Cassie. They're jealous.'

'Jealous?'

'Because she's popular with guys. Because she's cool.'

'Do you really think Cassie's cool?' Jodie was halfway between pissed-off and pitying. 'Nobody thinks your friend is cool. Just sad and fucked up, really. The only reason she still talks to you is because you're the last person to believe she's cool. The big question is, why are you still talking to her?'

* * *

I called Cassie that night. Her cell phone was off, so I tried the landline, something I hadn't done in a long time. It was a surprise when Anders Shute answered — somehow all this time he hadn't remained real to me: upon hearing his quiet, smooth voice, I was stunned concretely to realize that all these months he'd been present in that house, in Cassie's house, every night at the dinner table and every morning fussing with the radio, his stray pubic hairs tangled in the drain, the vestige of his scent in her mother's bedroom.

'I'm afraid Cassie can't come to the phone,' he said.

'It's Julia,' I said. 'Do you know when she'll be home?'

'She's home,' he said. 'But she can't come to the phone just now.'

'I see,' I said, in a way that made clear that I didn't.

'It's a family rule,' he explained. 'Cassie needs to finish her homework before she socializes.'

I left him my number, although she knew it. A family rule? What did that mean? He wasn't family.

Cassie didn't call me back that night, and when we spoke about the rumor at school she was defensive and furious. She even seemed a little scared. 'That's gross, Juju. I can't believe you'd even *ask* me that.'

'I'm not asking if you did it, I'm telling you what people are saying.'

'Even to repeat it to me is like saying it's true.'

'I'm not repeating it to anyone else here, am I? I'm telling you, is all.'

She shook her head. 'Whose side are you on?'

'Are there sides?'

'Friends don't talk shit about their friends.'

'I *didn't*. I told them it was bullshit. But I thought you needed to know what's going around.'

She changed the subject. We talked instead about how hard she was finding math class, and whether she should get some tutoring help. She showed me a photo in *Seventeen* of a two-hundred-dollar leather backpack that she wanted for her birthday and knew she wouldn't get.

'If only my dad were around,' she said, 'he'd get it for me.'

I remembered Shute's voice on the phone the night before, acting like he was her father. 'I bet you miss him.'

'Baby you have no idea,' she said in a theatrical voice, and flipped through the magazine to a feature about One Direction. 'Which one's for you?' she asked. 'Harry Styles is definitely hot, but I feel like he's the most obvious choice, don't you? Like, he's the default setting.'

Later I tried to have a repeat of the One Direction conversation with my mother, who always wanted to try to seem younger than she was. She went along with it for about five minutes and then fake-screamed and pretended to tear her hair out. 'The inanity!' she shrieked. 'I can't bear the inanity!'

'What do *you* want to talk about then?'

'How about the presidential race, and the fact that we're going to elect our nation's leader — either the same one or a new one — in about six months? How about we talk about that, instead of One Direction?'

'Do we have to?'

'It matters, sweetie. We have to.' She then made me listen to a political program on the radio, and over dinner with my father, we discussed it, like having social studies class at home. I was surly and annoyed, but I did it.

* * *

Peter Oundle was also interested in politics, it turned out, and when I mentioned the radio program, he'd heard it too, not because anyone told him to but because he liked that sort of thing. He gave me tips about online magazines to check out, because their coverage of the issues was, he said, 'really sharp.' In the way I might have looked up bands recommended by an attractive boy — not expecting, really, to like the music, but feeling it was an essential homework of flirtation, what my mother called erotomorphia, an illness she attributed to half of America's teenage girls — I looked up the journals online. The articles weren't totally engrossing, but they weren't intolerable either.

He told me to watch a film called *Gasland*, that he said explained fracking. I could see that the issues Peter cared most about — nature and the environment, fracking, and the global-warming discussion — were bigger than our own individual lives.

On some level, environmental issues felt abstract and remote, but I still thought I could make a passionate speech about the effects of global warming. So I went to Mr. Cartwright and suggested it as the topic for my final speech project of the year. It would mean moving categories, from 'Declamation and Recitation' to 'Original Argument,' an issue only because I was new to the team: usually it was the eighth graders who did Original Argument. But Mr. Cartwright gave me the thumbs-up, and told me I had two weeks to write the draft because the tournament was, by then, little over a month away.

He said that the best way to write a strong speech was to make it personal. Our house hadn't been flooded or destroyed by a tornado; no tree branches had fallen on our car. I could speak about my terror of thunder-snow — the first time I'd seen lightning in a snowstorm, I thought it was the apocalypse — but that wasn't particularly interesting. I could speak about the devastation of Hurricane Katrina, but that was ages ago — historical, really — and I'd never been to New Orleans. I could try to prepare something about the recent horrible earthquake in Japan — it had caused a nuclear accident too, just a year before. But I didn't have any personal connection to the event, for one thing; and for another, it wasn't simply a global-warming issue. While you could argue that it was caused by global warming, you couldn't reduce it to that.

My father reminded me about Rudy the caretaker. 'Remember that freak storm a couple of years ago? Hurricane . . . who? Which was it?'

'I don't remember,' my mother said.

'A girl or a boy?' I loved that storms had genders.

'I can't tell you. The point is, it was a freak storm, a late hurricane, shouldn't have been this far north. They'd predicted coastal flooding and everyone boarded up and evacuated along the beach, but then it mostly didn't turn out as badly as they'd feared.'

'Mostly?'

'High winds and rain, the kind that makes the road flood in twenty minutes, but bursts of it, not consistent.'

'I remember,' my mother said suddenly. 'That string of mini-tornadoes, right? What was the name for those things?'

'Damned if I remember.'

'I can look it up just now on my phone,' I said. At that point I was the only one in the family with a smart phone. 'What's it? A name for a mini-tornado?'

'It's not *quite* a tornado,' my father said. 'It's *like* a tornado.'

'What are you doing with your phone at the table?' My mother raised her voice. 'We made rules about that thing.'

'It's not *at* the table, it's *near* the table.'

'And that makes it acceptable?'

'Let her look it up. It bugs me that I can't remember.'

'Oh, for heaven's sake!'

'A dust devil? Is it?'

'No. Keep going.'

'Rich! We're at table!'

'You wouldn't stop her going to get the encyclopedia, would you?'

'But — '

'But she wouldn't be able to find it there, because she doesn't already know the word.'

'Derecho?'

'Bingo! That's it. Thank you, Miss Julia. A string of derechos. What does it say about them?'

'They're thunderstorm wind events, but are not tornadoes. 'These storms produce strong straight-line winds and can cause damages similar to a tornado.' '

'See? That's exactly right. I remember having the conversation with Rudy about it, in the Rite Aid parking lot. He explained all that to me. Caused by the hurricane. A string of derechos. Sounds Mexican, Doritos and nachos put together. He was disappointed, as if there would've been more cachet in a tornado. A higher class of storm.'

'Dad — '

'The point is, a derecho destroyed his house. A little clapboard Cape in the woods out the Vine Tail Road by the nature reserve. He'd lived there with his mother and as I recall, she'd died not long before, so it was especially devastating. I went out and saw it, with Eric, at the time

— flattened, like a giant had stomped on it.'
'Where does he live now?'
'Same place.' My dad got up to clear the table.
'Rich! That's Julia's job.'
'Give the kid a break. I'm finishing my story.'
'Did he rebuild the house?'
'No, he brought in a double-wide and set it on a raised concrete foundation. Real backwoods stuff. Basically what he could afford with the insurance. Primitive. He keeps that dog in a pen outside, and I've heard that at night she howls like a werewolf.'
'That's a great story, but it doesn't help Julia with her speech.'
'Did the derecho blow the house down? Or was it a tree falling?'
'You can ask him. But the storm tore up a line of old pines like they were matchsticks — it's still there, like a road cut through the forest — and I guess the house was in its path. A twisted pile of firewood with some mud-soaked furniture strewn about. When I went out there, that's what it was.'
My mother sighed. 'Not very cheerful.' She took the vanilla ice cream out of the freezer. 'I think we need a Parisian moment. Poire Belle Hélène, anyone? I'll heat the chocolate sauce, if you'll change the subject.'
'I think you should interview Rudy,' my dad said. 'His story will make a great speech.'
'But was it global warming that caused it?' I asked. My mother put the pears in bowls and scooped the ice cream.
'Of course it was. Who ever heard of a

hurricane — or a derecho, for that matter — this far north in November before?'

'I hear you,' my mother said, 'but it's dinnertime, and Rudy can wait. Sweetie, why don't you tell us about the lacrosse game this afternoon? Who won?'

* * *

This was how I came to interview Rudy Molinaro about his house. It made him into a sort of ally. I didn't know any adults that weren't related to kids I knew, or to school, so he was a first. Rudy made being an adult seem weirdly like being a kid — as if things happened to you, and you couldn't really change the course of life. Like it was fated, somehow.

My dad took me over to Rudy's on a Sunday afternoon, and sat on a bar stool by the kitchen counter reading the newspaper while I interviewed Rudy with my mom's old pocket tape recorder — 'the tools of the journalist's trade,' she'd said as she rummaged in her desk for it and waved it triumphantly aloft.

'I know you,' Rudy said when we arrived. He pointed his stubby finger at me. 'You go with that little blond girl. Hair white as an angel. I seen you around town.'

'Not so much anymore,' I said. 'But yeah.'

My knees almost touched Rudy's on the little brown corduroy sofa. A cigarette burn in the cushion next to my thigh distracted me: inside the hole I could spy tufty yellow foam and my fingers wanted to worry and pick at it. Finally I sat on my right hand to stop.

Rudy's story was sad. He'd grown up in the house in the woods, and after high school he'd done an electrician's apprenticeship with a firm over in Lawrence, and had eventually saved enough to move out of his parents' place and rent an apartment in downtown Royston. This made him the first Royston apartment dweller I'd ever knowingly met. For a time, he'd had a girlfriend, and they talked about getting married, but she wanted to move to Boston, and he wanted to stay near home, where he knew everyone and everyone knew him. Then his dad had a heart attack while driving and crashed the pickup on the interstate, aged fifty-nine, and Rudy, himself aged thirty-one and single (the girlfriend having made her move), was faced with a tough choice.

Home alone in the woods, his mother, diabetic, had a bad leg, so she couldn't drive. She couldn't have moved to an apartment in town, where there would've been stairs. So Rudy moved back into the house on Vine Tail Road, and he got Bessie the German shepherd instead of a bride, and he loved her just as much, even though she wasn't allowed to sleep in the house with him. Rudy spent most of his thirties there — he'd been let go from the electricians' outfit in Lawrence in 2009, when the recession hit and they were downsizing, though he was the last employee not to be a blood relation of Doug Bergdahl, the owner and founder, and Doug had made much of how sad he was to see him go.

After that, it was odd jobs, and the security

guard-cum-maintenance post for the Land Association, whose land included the asylum — a basic income boosted by short cleanup contracts, which didn't pay too well, but for God's sake, it was a job, they weren't easy to come by, and it enabled him to look after his mother. She was deteriorating from the time he came home to her — missing his dad is what Rudy said, but later my father suggested that Mrs. Molinaro had been fond of a drink or two, which, he explained, is an even bigger problem when you're diabetic. It got so she was essentially bedridden, and then Rudy became a bit teary remembering and we didn't go into much detail, but he said that hospice had been great, he didn't know what he would've done otherwise, and by that he meant specifically Bev Burnes. I could picture it, even though the double-wide where we sat and drank instant coffee obviously wasn't the same as the vanished Cape, but I imagined it similarly uncleaned, with gritty carpets and dust balls and sticky rings on all the surfaces. I could see the bustling, voluminous, righteous Bev, crackling down the drive in her Civic, stethoscope dangling from her neck, ruddy-faced and a tad wheezy in her cloud of sweet scent with her candy fingernails aflutter as she made order, a little derecho of cleanliness in the house, wiping a surface, soothing a brow, taking a pulse, changing a diaper, and eventually — the Angel of Death — administering her seductive and essentially fatal morphine.

In all this busyness, Rudy would have been baffled and grateful, grateful. He was not — he is not — what my mother calls *reconstructed*, nor what she calls *sophisticated* either. Bev would have seemed to him like a lighthouse on a rock, a sturdy and gracious illumination that transformed his dark corner of Royston.

His mother died of a stroke — 'a mercy,' he said that Bev had said, 'because you knew her path was headed in one direction only' — in March of 2010, when there were not yet any signs of spring on the forest floor, or birds to sing consolingly in the branches, and Rudy had felt very alone, except for Bessie, who howled for three days straight as if to purge his grief.

So when the storm had come late that fall and flattened the house, destroying what remained of his known life, the devastation was complete. He didn't say that — he wasn't the kind of person who would say such a thing; in fact, he looked at his hands and mumbled, 'It was bad. Real bad,' and for a full three minutes afterward said nothing more (I watched the digital clock on his stove in the silence, exchanged glances with my father, waited), as if letting those few words blossom into the room around us, the full and inexpressible badness of his loss. I gathered that he'd felt some dark justice was at work, that he was losing the material objects that represented what he'd already lost with his mother's death, as if nature were forcing him to understand that he needed to begin again from the beginning, that nothing, ever, would be the way it had been before.

The night of the storm, he'd been at a poker game in town, a monthly gathering of old friends from high school. Because the bad weather was forecast, he'd taken Bessie in the truck — 'She hates a storm; all dogs do. They smell it before it comes,' he said — and had locked her in the cab, where she sat in the driver's seat with her nose to the steering wheel and her ears pricked. 'In the worst of it, I went out to check on her, and she was crying. Okay, but crying a lot. I'd been careful not to park near any trees, just in case. Falling branches, you know. But the crying broke my heart. So I asked Ham, could I bring her in, could she stay in the kitchen, and he said sure, so I did. But the crying didn't stop. With the guys, we laughed about it, a great strong dog like Bessie, afraid of a bit of weather. I thought it was the wind, you know? The sound of the wind.' He shook his head. 'But later . . . Ham had me stay till the storm calmed down, all of us stayed, a poker marathon — I lost a hundred bucks that night — and later, when I drove back to the house and saw . . . well, then I figured Bessie knew all along. I think she knew when it was happening.'

'It's a good thing you took her with you,' my father said.

'You bet.' Rudy smiled. One of his front teeth was gray, a dead tooth, so his smile had a bit of the jack-o'-lantern. And then he was missing some teeth farther back, so his mouth crumpled in some. He really wasn't scary, I could see up close, with his paunch and his stubby fingers and the wispy gray curls on top of his head. The skin on his cheeks was red and thick, but his dark eyes were like a dog's eyes, hopeful and sad.

'Wisest thing I ever did, taking Bessie that night.' I could see him imagining the other possibility. 'Not that,' he said, 'I don't think I could've stood it. She's what I've got,' he said. 'She's my family. My wisdom.'

I thought back to that late-summer afternoon, Cassie and I hidden in the asylum, peering down at him and Bessie and the truck, and how I'd been sure that she knew we were there. 'They're smart dogs, German shepherds, aren't they?'

'Smarter than most people,' he said. 'Than most people I know, anyhow.'

Then I remembered how I'd imagined that with his loud Springsteen music, he was reliving a carefree youth; but now I could see Rudy up close, I knew that couldn't have been the case. He'd never been that guy, sure of himself, his arm around a girl in the cab of the truck. I knew the younger versions of guys like him at school, awkward, lonely, a bit slow, gravitating toward other boys like themselves for the relief of companionship, hoping for and expecting little, and grateful, grateful, for what they got.

* * *

The speech came out well — 'a near ideal combination,' according to Mr. Cartwright, of the personal and the scientific. I chose a few details from Rudy's story — tear-jerking details, like the moment, the morning after the storm, that he found his mother's favorite photo of her and his dad when they were young, mud-soaked in a tangle of wet branches and debris. For all that Bessie's apparent intuition made a great story and was the most meaningful part to me, it didn't have much to do with global warming, so I left it out. You've got to shape the story into an argument, Mr. Cartwright told us, and that means you choose what to put in, and what not to. I started with Rudy, expanded out to Hurricane Katrina and other, bigger, weather events, and then got going with my statistics. Mr. Cartwright always told us that we respond to the individual, not the collective — that we get more upset about one specific child's death than about the news of 500 or 1,000 dead people — and I kept that in mind. I may have made Rudy sound more heroic and stoic than he was in real life (in real life, my father suggested, it seemed that since his mother's death Rudy had struck up his own friendship with Johnnie Walker's poor cousin), but it helped to get my point across and I didn't make anything up. Mr. Cartwright said he thought the speech would stand a good chance at the tournament, which was as high praise as he gave anyone, so I was happy. In the end, I came in third, but the kids who did better were both eighth graders, so it still felt like a triumph. Jodie, who was in a totally different category, performing a monologue from *The Taming of the Shrew*, was even a bit jealous.

⋆ ⋆ ⋆

It's funny what time does: each day a drop of water, and without you realizing it, the stone below the drops wears a smooth divot. By late spring, I didn't think too much about Cassie. I didn't never see her, but we didn't hang out. Peter Oundle had become my friend rather than her boyfriend, and if their failed romance was the reason, then I was grateful to Cassie. Even though he adored her, and maybe loved her even more after they broke up, I knew she could never have been right for him: sure, he ran the 400 meters and was invited to all the parties, but at heart he was a poet, and he showed me his poems and talked to me about them, and asked my opinion about words and lines. For some, he composed music, made them into songs — these, unlike the others, usually rhymed — and he tried them out on me too. He invited me around to his house — the first time, I got nervous, as though it *meant* something; but it quickly became clear there wasn't anything particularly meaningful about it, for him anyway.

Peter had a keyboard and a guitar in his room, and he'd play and sing for me, and we'd work on the lyrics together. I'm not a trained musician, but I know, somehow, how a song should go, the way I know how a story should go, the way I can anticipate the plot of a TV show before it unfolds and I'm almost always right. He said nobody else could do it the way I could, that we were collaborators. He said he kept forgetting that I was younger than he was, because I gave such good advice and seemed so wise. I tried hard not to let his praise feel like it meant something else.

I couldn't imagine him ever doing these things with Cassie, or praising her in this way. But he carried a torch for her — for some fantasy of her anyhow — and even as I searched for a glimmer of romantic interest from him, I couldn't find it. The way his eyes went soft, and his voice, when he spoke about Cassie, I knew he still loved her. He had a habit too of rubbing his left index finger with his right thumb when he talked about her, as if he were consoling his very hand, consoling himself, like it was hard to talk about her even though he wanted to. Otherwise, with me, he was easy and free: no long glances, no awkward silences, no fumbled gestures. Of course I looked for them — I hoped for them; I remembered how his hand, so briefly on my shoulder, had burned, that long-ago summer morning — but there was nothing.

Peter told me more than once how lucky he felt to have so close and smart a female friend. 'You're a rock,' he said. He told me all kinds of things — about how his mom drank too much, not strictly a drunk but one glass of wine too many, too often; and how she yelled at his dad, and how he hated it and felt sorry for her at the same time. He told me about his older brother's severe dyslexia — Josh was five years older, and in college — and how he'd never done well in school and was struggling to get through UNH, 'on the eight-year plan,' Peter said, quoting his dad with a rueful smile; and how disappointed his parents were in Josh, how they looked to Peter to make up for it. He told me about his insect phobia and his childhood asthma, about loving old music like Bob Dylan, and Japanese anime. He showed me tons of photos of Tokyo on the computer — he dreamed of going there.

He talked to me about anything and everything, but like we were girlfriends, or old people. He was oblivious, either willfully or naturally, to my interest.

My mother said he'd figure it out in time: 'Don't be the *im*-patient!' she joked, although I had trouble cracking a smile at the allusion to Anders Shute, emblem of everything that had gone wrong.

* * *

From the spring of seventh grade to the fall of ninth grade is a long time. A lot happens. Some things happen fast, like a car accident or a heart attack; other things happen slowly, like the disintegration of a friendship or a marriage, or like cancer, and you don't even know they're happening, really, until the crisis comes, by which time it's too late.

With someone you've always known and have loved without thinking, there's the strangeness of knowing everything and nothing about them at the same time. At school, sometimes, we'd chat in the hallway or the cafeteria, and Cassie would make a certain face, or use a certain word, or run her hand through her hair a certain way, and I'd know exactly what she was feeling, and it would all still be there between us: you couldn't take away our whole lives. But our friendship was, at the same time, like a city you hadn't visited in a long time, where you know the streets by heart but the shops and restaurants have changed, so you can find your way from the church to the town square, no problem, but you don't know where to get ice cream or a decent sandwich.

Cassie and the Evil Morsel were close, all that time. They went to parties together at the weekends in the eighth grade. On Instagram, you could see they were at high school parties, and Peter — with whom I still spoke and texted and whom I saw regularly, even though he was at the high school campus in Royston — said when he saw them, after Homecoming or on Bonfire Night or the midwinter formal, the girls were always together, laughing loudly and cracking jokes about booze and weed. If they weren't partying, they wanted you to believe they were.

I couldn't figure how Bev allowed it. Maybe she was simply distracted by love. One time my family was out for Chinese at the Lotus Garden, a Sunday night, when Bev and Anders Shute came in for dinner. They stopped by our table and my mother asked them about Cassie, and Bev said she'd wanted to stay home and do her homework. I thought that was strange — she needed to eat dinner too, right? I figured that Bev and Anders Shute were happy to be together, and Cassie was happy to be without them. It seemed lonely, for a kid. Then it occurred to me she might not be alone, and that even if she was, she probably wasn't doing homework. I was in all honors classes and I didn't have *that* much homework. 'The devil makes work for idle hands,' Bev used to say when we were little, whenever she gave us chores to do. At that point it seemed as though the devil might be paying more heed to Cassie than Bev was.

What I didn't know until later — though I might have surmised it — was how tempestuous things had grown at the Burnes house. My father heard from Mr. Aucoin when he came in for his six-month cleaning, that one night well after dark he came across Cassie walking up the verge of Route 29 toward town, away from home. He stopped and told her to get into the car and he'd take her home, my father said that Mr. Aucoin said, and Cassie said, very politely, 'No, thank you. I'm going to a friend's house,' and Mr. Aucoin said, 'Well, if that's the case, at this hour your mother should take you there. You can't wander along the highway. So get in, and I'll take you home.' And she again demurred, and he said, 'Cassie Burnes, I am not leaving until you get into the car. But if you would rather, I'll call 911 and Officer Callaghan can take you home in the cruiser instead.' And then she got in the car, my father said Mr. Aucoin said, and he took her home.

I never heard Cassie's side of that story, which meant she didn't feel she could make a joke out of it. But I thought about what it would have been like, to be walking in the dark that way — she could only have been upset, right? Just plain running away, no destination, just away. Because why else would you? Unless Bev was on call and Cassie needed to go somewhere (but where? Delia's house was way too far. I couldn't imagine where she'd be walking — even my house was over a mile, and Peter's more than three times that) and didn't want to ask Anders Shute; or else they were both out and she was home alone and maybe it seemed no scarier to walk alone down the side of the highway than to be huddled by yourself — the cat, Electra, long vanished, by now, into the woods — in the little house down the cul-de-sac.

But whatever the reason she was walking there, what did it feel like when the car pulled over, the headlights turning onto you like a blinding heat, breaking from the chain of traffic, and the car — what car? You couldn't tell in the dark if it was familiar or unknown, not what kind or what color it was. Like a nightmare, the window rolling down, and a man telling you to get in, and only then do you realize that he's someone you know, he's your next-door neighbor, and relief washes through you like new blood, all at once, a change in the inner temperature of your body — except that then he's insisting you get *into* the car, the one thing your mother told you never to do, never to get into a car with a strange man . . . but he's not strange, he's Mr. Aucoin, big and hairy as a bear, you can see the fur on the back of his paw on the steering wheel, in the reflected light. Then there's a new, cold wash inside you: it *is* strange that he's insisting in this way — you don't know him well; you know his wife and dogs better — and haven't you been told that some high percentage of abductions are by people the victim knows? How is it you are in this situation by the side of the highway where a large man is maybe going to force you into his vehicle? He must weigh more than twice what you do. You don't stand a chance. And if you don't get into Mr. Aucoin's car, how long will it be before another car arrives, another window rolls down, and another man — a face you don't yet know, the face of your nightmares — insists in the same way? And then he says the thing about Officer Callaghan and you're reassured — he wouldn't refer to the policeman if he planned to kill you, would he? — and you give in, you get in. And the old leatherette of his Buick LeSabre is crackly but smooth too, and the vents are blowing hot air on your already burning cheeks, and he pulls the car out fast onto the road so it spits gravel, and you think as the seat belt bell is pinging, I've fucked up, I've fucked up, he's going to kill me after all, and you only really breathe again when he turns off the engine in the driveway, his belly in its pilled sweater tight against the steering wheel, and clears his throat in that characteristic way that you sometimes hear in the summertime through an open window, and he says, 'Now, do you need me to come and have a word with your mother? Or are you going to sort this out?' And for the first time he touches you, just lightly on the forearm, a touch you can feel through your jacket is as light as a father's, surprising from so meaty a man, and he says, with certain urgency, 'She needs to understand — *you* need to understand — that you can't go walking along the highway at night that way. It's not safe. Do you hear me?'

You nod and say thank you, politely, though again part of you wonders if he's a pervert even to think it's not safe for you. He doesn't have daughters; what does he know? And you get out of the car and wave back at him from your front door, where you let yourself into the yellow light, and see him nod at you, a curt sort of nod, that makes you wonder if he understands more than he lets on.

And then, afterward, there is the fleeting apprehension, the anxiety, that all the emotion and dread you experienced was a kind of pornography, a sort of made-up fear like the fear in games of pretend or in horror films, an almost erotic titillation bred in you by your deep understanding of how stories go, how they should go, and when a teenage girl walks alone in the night there is a story, and it involves her punishment, and if that punishment is not absolute — rape and even death itself — then it must, at the very least, be the threat of these possibilities, the terror of them. And that all the stories you've grown up with have made you feel, in that moment by the highway, not only like the victim but like the heroine in a story someone else will tell about you: this is a rare occasion when you are the star of the show.

All this I imagine for Cassie, even then, in the winter of eighth grade, so it doesn't matter that she didn't tell me, or anyone I know, about it, because I've lived it too. Although I wonder whether in Cassie's head, when the car pulled over, all she felt was irritation — what the fuck is it now? How much worse can this day *get?* — and whether she would've got into the car, whoever's car, and all the faster if it had been headed beyond, into the great, wild dark? We're different, Cassie and me, it turns out we always were, wanting to hold on to and let go of different things. Like the Janis Joplin song my mother loves — *freedom's just another word for nothing left to lose* — maybe already then, Cassie was ready for the next thing, even though she had no idea what it might be.

Now, of course, all this time later, I wonder why, when my father told me Mr. Aucoin's story, I didn't text Cassie, or call her even, or stop at her locker and ask her to talk to me. To be honest, I didn't even consider doing it. I shook my head and held the story inside. I didn't tell Jodie — why would I? I already knew what she would say — although I did tell Peter, and we talked a bit about it, and he wrote a song, a slow, mournful song about a girl by the side of the road at night, that I told him was his most beautiful one yet (it was); and as far as I know he never talked to anybody else about it.

But surely the reason Mr. Aucoin spoke, lying back in my father's dentist's chair, his open mouth vulnerable under a different set of bright lights and my dad's gloved fingers poking at his gums, the reason he told my father the story was because he knew Cassie and I had been friends forever, and he knew my father would tell me, and he thought that surely then the information would be in the right hands and someone, someone, would do something with it.

* * *

That summer I went away to summer camp for the first time. Mr. Cartwright recommended a theatre camp in upstate New York, on Lake George, where he'd taught when he was young. Jodie and Jensen were planning to do it too, but it turned out to be too expensive, especially for the two of them, so I went without knowing anyone. My parents drove me there, my gear in the back of the station wagon, and they forgave me for shooing them away almost as soon as we'd entered the camp gates. 'We'd think it was strange if you wanted to know us, bunny,' my father said — how could he call me bunny when someone might hear? — and my mother waxed sentimental. She'd loved camp as a kid — Archery! Canoeing! Campfires! — but also found this world of aspiring actors, many from New York, alien and a bit intimidating.

I loved it: the dusty cabins that smelled of old wood and the light on the water in the early mornings. Even the bad food and the slimy shower stalls with their industrial rubber curtains seemed part of the charm. Above all I loved the people, and the plays. I gouged a hole in my middle finger while striking a set, and even now I look at the thick white scar with pleasure and a little pride. I was as entertained as I was annoyed by 'the Teflon crowd,' a set of oddly good-looking almost-successful child actors with headshots at the ready and blue-white teeth. But they were a small proportion of the broader group that included six scholarship kids from inner-city Chicago, a Canadian farmer's daughter, and the heroically nerdy and myopic son of a trendy New York fashion designer. Forever pushing his bottle-bottom glasses up his bony nose, he was famous for his bad puns.

Our counselors too were an odd band of high school seniors and college kids who knew obscure monologues by heart. One girl, dressed like a druid, could recite all of Alexander Pope's 'The Rape of the Lock'; another had seen *Angels in America* fourteen times; still a third wandered around singing the songs from *Wicked* at top volume. The techies were computer wizards and master carpenters who could transform the stage into a downtown disco or the Forest of Arden, with colored lights, burlap, and painted plywood; and for a black-box production of *Cloud Nine* put on by a troupe of older campers, the set designer and her team constructed a raked diamond-shaped stage with checkerboard parquet — all in four days — that made the whole play seem like a fantasy from Lewis Carroll.

There was, in that place, a different social order, where particular skills — solving a Rubik's cube in less than ten minutes; sewing a Maid Marian dress out of five yards of turquoise polyester chiffon and some Christmas ribbon; having perfect pitch or a photographic memory for lines or the ability to do accents of many lands — had way more social currency than good skin or an expensive pair of sandals.

It was my first year — some kids were on their fourth or fifth, even — and I didn't get the biggest part in my main play — I was the Nurse in *Romeo & Juliet* — but I did perform Ann in a staged reading of Albee's *At Home at the Zoo*.

And in truth, I had just as much fun being a props assistant on the musical.

That month, Royston fell away: for the first time I could picture myself elsewhere, doing something consuming and unexpected. It didn't seem impossibly beyond reach.

When I came home, I kept telling my parents and friends stories about camp. They smiled and pretended to listen, but I could see their eyes glaze. I sent too many emails and texts to my new camp friends, and was as thrilled to receive their replies as if each were a new boyfriend.

In August, I went with my parents for two weeks to a rented house on Mount Desert, where we went boating and hiked in Acadia National Park and swam in the freezing sea. I read, and started writing a play I never finished — about two friends who go camping together and one of them gets injured — and I planned all the ways I'd be different in high school, how I could transform myself: be an actress, maybe start a rock band. I started listening to Amanda Palmer, a favorite of Shu-Lee, my bunkmate at camp. I decided I'd start wearing eyeliner, dress differently — vintage seemed right, some combination of '50s or '60s dresses and work boots. I asked my mother if I could get my hair cut in Portland, or even Boston, somewhere more sophisticated and trendy than the Supercuts next to the Target in Haverhill, and she said sure, she'd take me to the city before Labor Day.

We made a girls' outing of it, manicures and lunch at the Copley Plaza in addition to the haircut, done by a young guy with at least six piercings on his head alone, and his arms so brightly and fully tattooed that you could hardly see any bare skin. Once he layered my dark curls, the shape of my head looked different, and my face appeared delicately rounded rather than blockishly large. He'd been able to see my vision of my actress self — tough but soft, outgoing but cool — without having to be told. Like he *got* me, somehow. He assured me I had gorgeous eyes, which meant a lot to me even though he was gay and talked nonstop about his new boyfriend. My mother didn't have her hair cut, but she did buy a peacock-green cocktail dress in a boutique on Newbury Street after trying it on twice — both before and after lunch — and agonizing mildly about the price.

'Where will I wear it?' she fretted. 'It only makes sense if I wear it.'

'You can wear it to sleep in, if you like,' I said. 'You can wear it to any dinner party. It's not *that* dressy.' I could tell she really wanted it and needed to be given permission. My mother veers between extravagance and unexpected stinginess. When she's putting out disintegrating leftovers for the third day in a row, she refers to her own parents' wartime childhoods as if that explained it; and she'll persist with the slippery nub of soap at the sink until it's too small to hold. But she can turn around and blow hundreds of dollars in a single day on things that aren't, strictly speaking, necessary. She calls this spontaneity. She's probably worn the dress three times.

I was pleased to see her get the dress, and we

ate lobster salad off white linen for our ladies' lunch, and I felt beautiful and new after the care of the tattooed stylist. On the way back to Royston in the car, I said to her, as we looked out at the highway (even the interstate verges were rendered beautiful by the mottled late-afternoon sun) that I felt thankful for our day together, and fortunate that she was my mother.

* * *

I didn't speak to or see Cassie until after school started, ninth grade, back in downtown Royston in the high school building we'd walked past and played around for so many years. Although she hadn't grown much — she was probably 5′2″, and still so thin — the proportions of her face had changed. Her nose was broader, her forehead higher, the arc of her cheek-bones more deliberate. She had an adult face, one that looked as though it should be on a woman of six feet, not on a doll-sized person. No longer scrappy-looking, as I'd always known her, she'd become beautiful. Beautiful in a way that revealed my fancy haircut as a hoax, because with Cassie there was nothing to embellish or distract from her features. Her hair hung down, eternally fine and pale, below her shoulders; and either she'd become so expert with the makeup that she knew how to apply it invisibly, or she'd renounced it altogether. Her skin, lightly freckled, was like cream sprinkled with cinnamon. Her perfection made the gap between her teeth look like the handiwork of a marketer who, aware that perfection repels, had arranged, cannily, for this one alluring flaw.

Her expression too had changed. She looked like an adult, yes, but a melancholy adult, as though great burdens had fallen upon her in the months since last we'd met. Her eyes, always saucy and impish, were wary now, withholding. She was oddly friendly on the first day, and ran across the forecourt outside school to throw her arms around me. 'Juju!' she cried out, 'I've *missed* you!'

I couldn't relax in her embrace. Jodie told me at recess that the Vosul family had moved up to Maine — that foolish mother had got some job in Portland — and so Delia was gone.

'So you're telling me that Cassie is suddenly short of friends.'

'Could be.'

* * *

Cassie and I had lunch a few times in the cafeteria, with other kids around. She hung around with the same crowd as in the previous couple of years — the Evil Morsel's crowd, sans Morsel — but without her closest friend, Cassie didn't belong in the same way. I'd always thought of her as a renegade, not a leader but an independent spirit; but watching Cassie that fall, I had a different sense: that she was small and distressed and fierce in her distress — that the devil-may-care act was a response to her powerlessness, a 'better jump than get pushed' bravado. She was beautiful now, but she was also more clearly a wound, a wound trying hard to look like something else.

She came to my house, one afternoon in late September. From the high school we could just walk; it wasn't planned. As we lugged our backpacks through town, she phoned Anders — she called him Anders now — and told him not to pick her up; she'd make her own way home. His voice down the line sounded petulant, higher than I'd remembered. He dogged her a bit, about homework and getting dinner ready, but he didn't yell or anything. When she hung up she made an exasperated sound in her throat. 'Asshole.'

'How's it going, with that?' I asked, with an effort at bland concern.

'Don't patronize me, Juju.'

'I wasn't.'

'It's okay, I get it. As my mom and Shute say, the world separates the wheat from the chaff. It's from the Bible. They've already given up on me.'

'Don't be crazy.'

'You think so? My mom says I'll never amount to anything, and Anders — well, he'd do anything he could to stop me.'

'What's that supposed to mean?'

She shook her head. 'Nothing. It doesn't mean a thing.'

'Are you trying to tell me something?'

'I love you, Juju — you're so cute. If I was trying to tell you something, I'd tell it to you. No, just stating the facts.'

'We've got our whole lives.'

'Have you seen what that looks like in this

town? Clipping hair at the Mane Event? Working the line at Henkel?'

'We're both going to get out. You don't have to get far from here to see that the world is huge and full of crazy shit.'

'Correction: we'll both get out, but I've got to make my own way. I've got to make a plan.' She took a deep breath, and the words came in a rush like steam from a kettle. 'Do you even know what I did this summer? Summer school in math. Babysitting for the Callaghans and the Justices — that obnoxious little kid Jackson, still in diapers, having tantrums in public where he lies down and waves his arms and legs like a bug and screams for his mom. Fucking awful. That, and watching *Modern Family* on demand, trying to make sure the a-hole didn't catch me, because if you can believe it, he disapproves! You went off to your fancy camp and to Maine with your parents, and it was like I was in prison for three months. I couldn't wait for school to start — me, Cassie Burnes, can you believe it? I couldn't wait to get out of the house.'

At that point we reached my place. My mother was bringing groceries in from the car, so we helped her. She made a fuss of Cassie and how happy she was to see her ('We've *missed* you, you know,' she said emphatically, trying to look meaningfully into Cassie's eyes) and how she hoped we'd see more of her now that we were in town at the high school.

'Wander over anytime,' my mother said. 'Consider us a second home.'

'Sure thing. Thanks, Carole.'

We clattered up the stairs to my room at speed, as if we were having fun, making a familiar percussive thunder unheard in the house for years.

'Careful, girls.' I could hear from my mother's voice that she was smiling.

What did we talk about? Peter, maybe a bit. Other kids at school, teachers. We watched videos on YouTube — pop music and rap, but also comedy shorts like Eddie Izzard, Key and Peele, superficial stuff, a few laughs, but nothing between us that mattered. Then my mother called up to say she was heading out to pick something up and did Cassie want a ride home, and that was that.

If my mother thought it would be the first visit of many, she was mistaken. Cassie was friendly enough at school, as if I didn't have ice shards in my heart, as if I couldn't possibly; but she must have sensed something. Either that or she chose to keep a distance. I would not, could not, make a significant overture. My pride depended on this. She would have needed to make the effort, enough to be openly vulnerable; she would have had to risk my revenge. I like to think I wouldn't have rebuffed her, but it's possible that I would have. It's possible that I would have felt the need to exercise the power if I'd had it. But she didn't grant me the opportunity.

'She's so plastic,' I complained to Peter, who also spoke to her only at school. 'Like she's a cyborg. The real girl who was my friend all those years has gone over to the dark side.'

Peter sighed. 'She's got problems.'

'How do we know?' I knew he was right, but still.

'The very fact that she doesn't *want* us to see. You don't hide if you don't need to. It's like a planet: you know it has to be round, but you only see a crescent, or half a circle. So you infer that part of it is in shadow. Then you have to figure out what's in the shadow, and what causes it.'

'But what if there's just no *there* there?'

'That's crap, Juju.' It was.

'Anders Shute,' I said.

'What about Anders Shute?'

'Anders Shute is the shadow.' We talked about this. 'Though maybe,' I offered, 'the person she really hates is Bev; only that's not allowable, so Anders is the scapegoat.'

'Maybe. It seems more complicated than that.'

'You don't think he's doing anything bad, do you?'

'How do you mean?'

'You know what I mean.'

'Why would you even suggest that?'

'That shit happens, you know.'

Peter frowned. 'Did she say something?'

'Not exactly.'

'You've got to be careful, Juju. You can't go saying — even thinking — stuff like that. It's dangerous.'

'Okay. But what if *he's* dangerous? What if he's the Dark Thing?'

'What?'

'What if she needs our help to fight him?'

'She'd have to ask for help, you know? Short

of that, we'd be stirring up trouble where maybe there isn't any.'

'But what if — '

'You can't make a case on 'what if,'' he said, more certain now. 'My mom's a lawyer, and she always says that. Unless Cassie tells you something — or me, which doesn't seem likely — then it's conjecture. Which is to say, it's nothing at all. Don't go repeating that idea to anyone, okay?'

'Okay.'

'Not to your mom, or Jodie, or anyone. It's not a joke.'

'I know.'

I didn't take it lightly. But once I had it in my head, I couldn't entirely get rid of it. It felt logical, somehow. I read the papers. I watched TV. That kind of shit went on all the time, almost in plain sight. He was essentially a stepfather, wasn't he? And if wicked stepmothers had the worst rap in all fairy-tale history, stepfathers had the worst rap, as far as I could tell, in real-life history: they had all the power of a father, without the constraints. And if not Anders Shute, what was making Cassie into a half moon?

* * *

The next time she came to my house after school was in late January. A snowstorm blew in in the late morning, earlier and stronger than had been predicted: classes and practices were cancelled from one o'clock onward. Bev and Anders were still working, and Cassie had no way to get home, so I suggested that she come to my place. She asked a couple of other people before she agreed, but they lived farther away. So we walked back through the snow, the wind biting at our noses and cheeks.

I reminded her of our best sledding winter, when we were eight or nine, and of the snow fort we'd built in my yard with my father's help — a real igloo, nicely packed smooth — how we'd crawled inside with hot chocolate my mother made us and my sparse bag of leftover Halloween candy. We loved the igloo so much, wanting to pretend we weren't freezing, that we stayed there until we couldn't feel our toes. Afterward, we'd taken a steaming bath in the big Victorian claw foot, half laughing, half crying at the burn in our thawing extremities. It was probably the last time we'd been fully naked together. Even then I'd been slightly shy, aware of being a big-boned giant in the porcelain tub.

We were almost conspiratorial, remembering. When we got to my house and my mother was out, we made hot chocolate for old time's sake, and sat on the barstools in the kitchen to drink it. The snow came down in fast little flakes, almost sideways in the wind, the kitchen illuminated by its white light. Our faces tingled from the heat after the cold — 'a healthy glow,' my mother would say — and I could see Cassie's scalp pink through her snowy hair.

We felt so close, kicking our feet against the cabinets under the island, sticking our noses in the hot-chocolate steam.

'What's going on with you?' I asked. 'I mean, really?'

'What's that supposed to mean?'

'I only get the sunny side, nowadays. You may not notice it, but it's true. And I know there's stuff going on.'

'You do?'

'C'mon, Cass. How long have we been friends?'

'Are we still friends?'

'Aren't we?'

Her face was suddenly serious. 'We're friends, of course we are. Remember the Girl Scout song?'

'Sure I do.'

'So you're my gold friend. My goldest friend.'

'But?'

'But what?'

I looked away. 'But nothing,' I said, and turned back to her, and smiled a good fake smile.

PART THREE

Cassie disappeared in early April of ninth grade. She disappeared not once but twice, although from the outside, the two incidents seemed like one.

Some things I wrote down in my diary. I know that on the ninth of April, about a week after Easter, people were talking about it at school. It was a Tuesday. Cassie had gone missing on the Friday night or Saturday, apparently, but Bev and Anders didn't report it, not straightaway. There'd been an argument — she'd broken curfew on the Friday night and didn't come home until two in the morning — and Anders, according to Peter, who heard it from Cassie in the brief moment she was back, threatened to throw her out of the house for good.

'Out of *my* house!' Cassie had said to Peter, red-eyed and still wild about it. 'Can you believe that? Standing in *my* kitchen in his Jockey shorts at two in the morning, that pimply white chicken breast with his wispy chest-hair goatee between his tits, standing there telling me I'll lose my right to my own fricking house?!'

Bev, apparently, remained up in their bedroom while Anders yelled at Cassie. 'My own mother doesn't give a shit?' she said to Peter, incredulous even days later. 'After all I've put up with, day after day of it, over two years now, biting my tongue every single day, all for her, and she can't be assed to drag herself downstairs for me?' And again: 'I half wondered — no, fuck it, I totally wondered — if she'd sent him. Do you know what I mean? Can't you see it? Fluffing her hair with her fingers, all flirty, like 'Oh, Cassie, she's so out of control, I can't handle it, Anders honey, off you go!' All that bullshit about how we were a team! All my life, 'Just you and me, Cassie! We can do anything as long as we're together, Cassie! You're my one and only, Cassie!' That fucking lying fat cunt! All bullshit, all lies. From the get-go.'

Cassie had come to Peter, she told him, because he was the one friend she could trust. He was beyond surprised when she showed up — they hadn't hung out in ages — although he told me that after only a few minutes it felt like no time had passed. She told him that she knew he loved her — I rolled my eyes at that one, we all did; he hadn't gone out with any other girls after Cassie — and she knew that he was strong and sane. Peter told me he felt relieved, in a way, that at last it seemed like she could see him clearly. Peter wouldn't try anything, she knew, she said, and he didn't. But still, when Peter tried to put his arm around her — just as a friend, he told me, just consolingly — she flipped away fast and angry and lay on his bed facing the wall. She was that upset.

He couldn't say anything and he couldn't touch her. He listened to her staggered snotty breathing, and they waited, she and he, quiet like that, like she was an animal injured in a trap, and he watched the light fading at the window, the still-icy blue dusk, her eyes writ in the sky, and he sat on the floor with his knees up and his back against the side of the bed, and he waited, and waited, and eventually the breathing evened out and she was asleep.

* * *

This wasn't the story, of course; it was the hiatus in the drama — in Cassie's real-life drama, so far from a game of pretend. She slept on his bed in her clothes, without stirring, from that late Wednesday afternoon until late Thursday morning. He didn't tell his parents. He pretended to be sick, and skipped dinner, went downstairs only to say he was going to bed, and he stayed near her, eventually sleeping on the floor with a cushion beneath his head. She'd made him promise, when she arrived, that he wouldn't tell Bev she was there; which meant that Peter's parents couldn't know, or they'd insist. Cassie was an official missing person, after all.

'But you have to understand,' he said to me, 'she said it was life or death; she said, she insisted, that it would kill her to go home.'

'That *they'd* kill her?' I asked. When Peter and I had this conversation, Cassie had gone missing again, was missing, we realized, for real (though the first time had felt real too, until she came back). We had no idea what had happened to her.

The official story — Bev's story — was that they'd had an argument, another argument, the hundred thousandth argument, and that Cassie had stormed off. It seemed almost certain that an argument was part of the truth, and almost as certain that it wasn't the whole truth. Surely, we thought, sinister Anders Shute must have a part in the truth.

'She didn't say that,' Peter insisted, 'she said *it* would kill her. Which kind of made sense once she told me the story.'

* * *

Cassie's story, according to Peter, was this: back in the winter, probably around the time that she had come to my house in the snowstorm, her life at the Burnes house had become unbearable. She couldn't do anything right — Bev and Anders and, it seemed, God himself conspired against her — and Cassie, without the Morsel, without me, without Peter, was on the verge of despair.

I try to imagine feeling lonely the way she felt lonely, then. I'm not sure that I can. I'm a dog and she was a cat: I, slobbery and keen; she, self-contained and ultimately private. For so many years it didn't matter; but then she was alone, in her feline nature, and lonely. I should have been able to sense how it was. She was too proud to tell me, or Peter for that matter; and I was too proud and too wounded to look.

But Cassie had always had her guardian angel. She'd always believed in him. He called her baby doll, he protected her from harm. He saw the sheen of her, where Anders and Bev saw only tarnish; she had faith in his faith. She wasn't crazy; she'd been told he was dead, but in order to find her path, her way out of Royston, she decided to search for Clarke Burnes, to see what she could find out.

She'd looked before. We'd looked together once, on my mom's computer, when we were younger. But she told Peter it had become a periodic thing, since Shute moved in, to check and see if she could find traces of her real father. She wanted to figure out, she said, who she was — and who she could become. She'd Googled his name a hundred times and there had never been anything that pertained. A Harvey Clarke Burnes of Rome, Georgia, and a Lucile Clarke Burnes, long deceased, and an Ann Clark Burnes, with no e, very much alive, with an account on Facebook. Documents involving a Mr. Clarke and a Mr. Burnes placed their names misleadingly side by side, so that they'd appeared on the search and caused her heart to beat faster for a minute. But this time, in the winter of 2013, when she Googled Clarke Burnes, she found — not on the first page of results, but on the fifth — a reference to an Arthur Burnes: 'Coach' Arthur Burnes, 'aka Coach, aka Captain Clarke, aka Cap'n Crunch.' It was the caption to a photo in the *Bangor Daily News*, of Bangor, Maine, from a few months before, when the Bangor High School football team had won the league final. The image showed entire the football team, along with Arthur Burnes, aka Captain Clarke, their senior coach. He was also, she discovered when she typed in the name 'Arthur C. Burnes' along with

'Bangor,' a beloved math teacher at the city high school, where he'd taught for the past fourteen years.

She studied the photo from the paper; she zoomed in close. Captain Clarke was small and blurry; when she zoomed in he was larger but also blurrier. A burly man grinning, with a bald head, plump cheeks, and a close graying beard. His varsity jacket pulled taut over his belly. His arms, in the photo, looked short, slightly apish, crossed awkwardly over his chest. Was this the floppy-haired guy in the flannel shirt in front of a long-ago barn? Who could say? How could it be?

But imagine, imagine for a second what it felt like to Cassie, even the possibility — baffling, horrifying, miraculous — that the grinning Captain Clarke might be, could be, maybe, in that awful winter, couldn't *not* be the man she told Peter she'd never really, in her deepest heart, believed to be dead: her father.

Cassie didn't tell anyone about her investigations. Convinced that Anders spied on her phone and computer and checked all her searches and hacked into her accounts, she deleted this from her laptop and thereafter Googled Captain Clarke only from the school library. She told Peter that it was amazing what you could learn about someone if you did a little digging.

Arthur C. Burnes was forty-one years old, married since 2001 to Anna Maria Machado, thirty-six, a civil servant with the city of Bangor, working in the tax department. Cassie imagined he was a mild joker, that he liked his food. Anna Maria — Cassie decided she used both names:

why else would they both be listed? — was a great cook, lots of meat in sauce, and kindly, with a little accent, maybe rolling her *r*'s.

They had four kids, aged three to eleven, and they lived at 36 Spring Street in a pale-blue split-level ranch with a basketball hoop above the garage and, on the Google street view, what looked like a husky playing on the front lawn. The husky, of course, might just have been a neighborhood dog that wandered into the frame as the Google camera van drove by — a trespasser dog. Hard to say.

Cassie found herself over the months of February and March increasingly immersed in the lives of the Burnes family of Bangor. She spent many afternoons in the school library, which would have surprised people if they'd noticed; but the one person who did notice was Lee Ann Barrocca, the school librarian, unobtrusive and old-fashioned, who didn't want to invade Cassie's privacy or dissuade a growing academic interest by approaching her uninvited. So Miss Barrocca just observed Cassie over her half-moon glasses from the remove of the checkout desk, and smiled privately, imagining that her beloved library was saving another student's future, a fantasy she used to console herself whenever she discovered defaced books or obscene graffiti in the carrels.

Cassie, meanwhile, started a notebook, stashed always in her school locker to keep it from prying eyes at home, in which she recorded the facts as she understood them: she learned the kids' names from 2012 holiday snaps on Flickr, a series taken at the Bangor City Hall's Christmas drive, where the two elder Burnes kids — Jason and Marisol — had helped to hand out gaudily wrapped presents from beneath the enormous glittering tree, to celebrate the season's Toys for Tots campaign. In a later family photo from the same series — inconveniently minus Arthur Burnes — she could see all four kids: Jason, Marisol, Jennifer, and baby Brianna, a curly haired wisp in red-and-green tulle, along with their mother. Jason looked thoughtful and a bit shy, the beginnings of dark down on his lip: smart in school, a math guy most likely. Marisol was the opposite, all tooth when she smiled, and crinkly cheeks, the kind of girl who put bubbles on her *i*'s and exclamation points, and who actually clapped her hands when she was excited. Jennifer was hard to read — Cassie liked that, felt she was probably closest in spirit to Jennifer. Her expression was melancholy and she had dark smudges under her eyes. Anna Maria, their mother, dark-haired, plump, and small, wore her hair in a ponytail like a young girl, and a red sparkly Christmas sweater. She looked kind, but tired. Cassie imagined that when she got angry, she didn't yell at her kids; she spoke quietly to them in a tight voice — an acceptable kind of anger.

Cassie, she told Peter, dreamed about this woman, about these kids — her stepfamily — and from these two photographs, she fantasized entire afternoons in their company. I imagine she tried to find, in the kids' dark-eyed faces, traces of her own features — the ears, at least? The bones? She couldn't be sure. She couldn't find any other photos of Arthur himself; it was true that her father had supposedly been slim rather than heavy, but people changed, and a whole lifetime — her whole lifetime — had intervened. Had Clarke Burnes played football in college, or even high school? Cassie didn't know, couldn't ask her mother. She *never* discussed her father with her mother; if there'd been glimmers when she was younger, they were long over now. The familial darkness was complete.

Whether Cassie's expanding family fantasy of life with the Burneses of Bangor made the situation at home worse, or whether her home life was simply doomed to deteriorate, it's hard to say. But in those late-winter months, Cassie and her mother and Anders Shute lived on high alert, awaiting eruptions or trembling in their aftermath. We didn't understand at the time what it was like, but Cassie told Peter, in his room that day. Cassie lost her phone privileges; Cassie was grounded; Cassie had to move her computer into the dining room and do her homework there, so that the grown-ups could see what was on her screen at any time. Cassie's tone was disrespectful; Cassie didn't do her chores properly; Cassie's allowance was indefinitely suspended; the lock on Cassie's bedroom door was removed.

With so many problems at home, Cassie devoted more and more energy to her Bangor fantasy. This is what she told Peter, who told me. She figured out how you could get there, without a car — Greyhound to Boston from the Dunkin'

Donuts on Route 29 at 6:10 a.m., and then the express bus to Maine (first stop Portland, then on to Bangor and eventually Mount Desert). There was a youth hostel in Bangor, $29 a night for a bunk in a dorm (bring your own bedroll). The Burneses' house looked to be only two miles from the bus station, so she figured she could walk there. Whether or not there were sidewalks, she could just walk there and climb the driveway and ring the front doorbell. You wouldn't want to do that during the day — who'd be home besides maybe the husky, who might be no friendlier than the Aucoins' Lottie? You'd come at dusk, the early evening, when the first stars were out and football practice had liberated Captain Clarke, aka Cap'n Crunch, to his own kids, and you'd ask — what would you ask?

For a while, Cassie was stymied. 'Are you my dad?' was too bald. 'Do you know who I am?' a little aggressive. 'Does the name Bev Burnes mean anything to you?' was another possibility, but who knew how that might turn out. If, indeed, Clarke Burnes was alive and not dead as Bev had always insisted, then either he'd faked his death to get away, or else they'd broken up badly. The timing wasn't implausible — a breakup and a move to Maine; starting his math-teacher job at the high school around the time he was supposed to have quit the planet. A *math* teacher, so close to biology; the right age; the name; so close by, relatively speaking . . . surely this couldn't be coincidence? How about 'Have you ever gone by the name Clarke Burnes?' Or even: 'Do you know a Clarke

Burnes?' Maybe, she decided, she'd just have to play it by ear.

This is what she told Peter, who told me, or mostly. I know Cassie so well it's like they're my own thoughts, or my own thoughts about her thoughts. Now, so much later, it almost feels like I went through it with her, even though I didn't know until afterward.

Cassie kept Googling the weather in Bangor, looking up photos of the downtown streets in different seasons; trying to picture what life there might be like. She told no one. She didn't want anybody's opinion, certain that her guardian-angel father still guided her steps, watched over her, would make sure she'd take the right path. She didn't set her heart on flight — she was okay with keeping this relationship with Bangor in her mind, for a while — but then came the blowup with Anders at two in the morning, and she didn't feel, suddenly, that she had much choice but to go. The angel's voice spoke in her ear, and said, 'Baby doll, it's now or never.'

The irony about the fight with Anders was that Cassie wasn't late because she'd been partying, or fooling around with a boy. Peter said she was particularly upset about this — that Anders Shute wanted to punish even her good deeds, maybe especially those. She'd been with a girl named Alma, a new friend from the high school, talking her through her breakup with her boyfriend. Alma felt that life wasn't worth it, and Cassie had sat in her overheated, ill-lit kitchen on the other side of town drinking Diet Coke for hours, listening and cajoling, trying to help Alma look to a better future, to see the light. Alma's mom was an aide at an assisted-living place in Lawrence, on the night shift; and the girls were alone until Alma's older brother Ugo came home well after one in the morning and offered Cassie a ride back to her house. By then she'd listened a long time to Alma cry and lament and then seem to pull herself together only to break down again. Cassie didn't know Alma all that well and wasn't even sure she liked her that much, but she was proud of her own behavior that night. She'd gone home feeling strong and patient and generous and good — and pleased too, that Ugo hadn't hit on her, which all too many older brothers were disgustingly ready to do — until Anders loomed thinly before her in the dimly lit kitchen, waggling his long finger altogether too close to her face and condemning her as selfish and un-Christian and 'beyond the pale,' and threatening to kick her out. He implied she was a slut, though he didn't use that word exactly. And the way he looked at her — those narrowed eyes, the line of his mouth, the pulsing vein in his temple, the utter surreality that this ugly stranger behaved as though he had rights, like he was her boss, or her father — you can only take so much, she told Peter, and then you have to stick up for yourself.

With her school backpack crammed with clothes, a hand towel, a rolled-up sheet, a box of Wheat Thins and an apple, Cassie left the house on her bike at 4:40 a.m., and arrived at the Dunkin' Donuts by 5:10, which was still night. Nobody else was there besides the guy behind the counter, bleary and dirty-haired with wispy fluff on his chin. She ordered a large regular coffee — I can taste it, toothache sweet — and two glazed crullers, and she hunched at the back table against the wall with her hood up, peering at the odd customers who came through. I can feel the plastic table under her fingers, and hear the slight screech of the built-in chair when she swivels in it. The bus lurched into the lot right on time, in the still-dark, its lights beaming into the coffee shop; and as she climbed the steps into its hissing pneumatic maw, the money for the ticket crumpled in her fist, it occurred to her only fleetingly that she could stop, and go home, and begin the day as if this plan had never existed. Her bike was carefully hidden in the bushes at the back of the DD parking lot, chained to a sapling. She'd left a note on the kitchen counter that just said 'Back in a few days.' That way, she told herself, they'd know she was okay. It didn't mean they wouldn't chase her — Anders Shute was that spiteful; her mother that controlling — but that was their problem, not hers. If she floated above herself, then it seemed like a strange thing she was doing, an irresponsible thing, maybe even a dangerous one; but when she stood in her skin and felt the cold greasy metal of the bus at her fingertips, and the dig of the backpack straps through her parka, and saw the sulfurous glimmer of dawn on the horizon as the car lights flashed past on Route 29 . . . in her skin, Cassie had no doubts at all, and no fear either.

The journey to Bangor took the better part of

a day. She thought everything through as she went along: she bought round-trip tickets to be sure she wouldn't run out of money and get stuck. After the tickets, she had still almost $200, money she'd earned babysitting and helping Mrs. Aucoin tidy up their basement. She put $50 between her left sock and her shoe, so that even if she lost her wallet or, God forbid, got mugged, she wouldn't be destitute. Before she got on the Boston bus, she remembered to turn off her cell phone — by then, even she had an iPhone, and of course her nosy mother had the Find My Phone app, and while Cassie didn't mind them knowing she'd got on the Boston bus, putting them on the wrong scent, she didn't want to be traced beyond that. She knew her hair was noticeable — her hair had always been a beacon, not just for me — so as soon as she got off the bus at South Station, she went to the nice bathrooms in the train station next door, where she pinned her white blondness inside a knitted beanie so you couldn't see a single strand — 'like I was Orthodox Jewish,' she told Peter, 'or maybe Muslim' — and then she put on a pair of slightly damaged sunglasses from the sale bin at the CVS. She didn't return to the bus terminal until it was almost time; she knew that runaway kids hang out in bus terminals, and that bad things can happen to them there. Careful not to look aimless, she read a magazine intently at one of the tables in the train station food court while waiting for her bus — she had several hours to kill — and made her McDonald's fries last a very long time, waiting minutes between bites, so that she mostly ate them cold, their floury grease coating her tongue.

When she bought the Bangor tickets, she used the machines and didn't make eye contact with anyone, and strode purposefully to the right bay at the right time. The Maine bus, on a Saturday afternoon, had a fair number of customers, and although she'd hoped for a seat by herself, she saw it wouldn't work out. She chose to sit next to a college-aged girl with glasses and a violin case, because of all the options, that person seemed least likely to strike up conversation. Tired of pretending to read, and unable to listen to music because she didn't want to risk turning on her phone even with the cell service off, Cassie decided to pretend to sleep. She didn't have to pretend for long. When the violinist got off at Portland, nobody replaced her; so Cassie slipped to the window and slept the rest of the way, her skull in its woolly cap bouncing uncomfortably against the glass, and her tailbone sore.

From midafternoon Saturday, Cassie was in Bangor. This was the tricky part: she couldn't get herself noticed; she couldn't seem to be barely fifteen. Even seventeen would be okay, but not fifteen. She'd worried about this, in her weeks of planning, she told Peter, and had decided, if anybody asked, to say that she was in town to see her sick grandpa, a patient at the hospital — Anders Shute's old hospital; what were the odds? — and that her mom was on her way too but had had to deal with a crisis at work. She'd even thought of a name — Cassie Byrd — and a way to explain it, if anybody asked: that her dad,

Clarke Byrd, had died, which was why her mom's name was different, or she preferred to go by 'Byrd' as a way to remember him.

'Pretty cool, don't you think?' she said to Peter. 'I read that it's always best to keep your lies as close to the truth as possible. It's harder to get caught out that way.'

Peter said that in the moment she said this, given what she was telling him about Bev, and what Cassie firmly believed was Bev's amazing ability to lie to her daughter over a lifetime, the need to stay close to the truth seemed not so obvious. But never mind.

In the event, nobody official asked anything. The youth hostel occupied a sprawling Victorian house near the downtown ('Like Julia's, but, like, five times as big,' she told Peter) and it was obviously spring break somewhere because the front hall was crowded with young backpackers — grown-ups, Cassie said, but barely. She got put in a room with three Swedish girls, two of them, Anja and Linn, as fair as she was herself. The third, Inge, small and dark with big breasts and wide blue eyes to rival Cassie's, was the most talkative. Nineteen, speaking perfect English, they were friends from high school, taking time to travel before university. They'd come to the West Coast first and were making their way back east — just another week before they flew home; but they wanted to do some early spring hiking in Maine first.

Cassie told them her prepared story, and when they invited her to join them for dinner she excused herself, saying she was too sad about her grandfather — he was really sick, or she wouldn't have come alone — and that she just needed to rest. She pretended she'd already been to the hospital to see him, earlier that evening. The Swedish girls were very understanding.

'I lost my grandpa too, about three years ago,' Inge said. 'My mother's father, the same as you. He had no memory by then, didn't know who I was, but I remembered so well how he'd been when I was small and we would play horsey, on his hands and knees, he'd let me ride around on his back. So sad.'

And then: 'Does your grandfather have his memory? I mean, does he know who you are?' Anja asked.

Cassie had to decide in a hurry. 'Mostly,' she said, to cover her bases. 'Mostly he knows, but not always.'

'What's he sick with?' Linn's turn.

'A cancer. A bad one.'

'Where is it?'

'Spread. It's spread all over. It's in his lungs and his brain and other places too.'

They nodded quietly and looked at the wooden floor, and then Inge got up and patted Cassie on the knee. 'It's really good that you're here, then. He probably doesn't have very long.' And then the three Swedish girls filed out to find some dinner, leaving Cassie alone beneath a fluorescent panel on a plastic mattress with her lone sheet and hand towel for bedding, for supper her Wheat Thins and for entertainment the tattered magazine she'd read in South Station.

Cassie hadn't ever expected to go to Bangor on the weekend. This wasn't the way she'd imagined encountering Arthur Burnes and her stepfamily. She was also in the thick of her lie about her grandfather, and felt she couldn't be seen by the Swedish girls to loiter around the hostel when she should be at his bedside. But the girls, keen to hike, dressed by the time it was fully daylight, and slipped quietly from the room, leaving their belongings tidily rolled and stacked for their evening return. Cassie discreetly opened an eye to watch their preparations at one point, Inge's breasts dangling only a couple of feet from Cassie's face as she bent to pull on her pants, but hadn't let on she was awake. It was a hostel, not a Hampton Inn, she told Peter; she couldn't hang out there all day; and she'd almost convinced herself of her fictional grandfather at the hospital. So when she'd showered and dressed, she embarked purposefully, head down, stride sure, for Bangor General, as if getting there really was important.

The spring morning was chilly but bright, and the budding trees nodded as she passed. Forsythia bloomed in yellow bursts across the yards, alongside patches of crocuses and bluebells. To Cassie, these were signs of hope, blessings on her path. Two cherries, earlier than the rest, had begun to unfurl their frilly pom-poms, and she paused beneath them for a while, looking up at the patches of blue sky behind the pink. She told Peter she felt better than she had in months. The air in her lungs felt different, the slight chill of her fingertips and the breeze at her neck, the rosy hue of the sun through the petals . . . it was like being kissed, not in a romantic way, she said to Peter, but in the way your mother — or father — kisses you when you are small, and gently strokes your hair.

Carefully beanied, without sunglasses, she managed to spend the morning at the hospital, between the gift shop, the main lobby, and the gloomy cafeteria, where she ate a cup of minestrone, a ham and Swiss on rye, and a rice pudding — her first real meal since leaving home. The food was cheap, for which she was grateful, and the rice pudding — Kozy Shack — pleasingly familiar. She made a constant effort to look like she knew what she was doing — as un-waiflike as possible — and she got so caught up in acting her role that, she told Peter, who told me, she could picture her nonexistent grandfather, lying upstairs in one of those complicated beds, head up, knees up just a little, draped in a sheet and a blue-speckled hospital gown, bony arms punctured by tubes, hooked up to blinking machines, his sparse white hair askew and his eyes half-closed. She pictured his face, its jaundiced, freckled parchment, and his irritating way of clearing his throat every minute or two. She pictured a real guy, a composite of some of the old guys she'd seen that very morning, and she so convinced herself that he was real she could feel tears behind her eyes at the thought of his imminent death. She was ready, if anybody at the hospital should ask her, to describe this grandfather in great detail, and to hurry back to him — her only doubt, having studied the directory in the entrance, was whether he'd be in Geriatrics on Three West or Oncology on Five East. But in her hours in the hospital, nobody at all seemed to notice her; certainly nobody addressed her; as though she flitted through invisible, a familiar.

Only now, frighteningly, did she wonder whether her grandfather really didn't exist, whether he'd died long ago the way Bev had always said, or whether, like her father, he'd been killed off by Bev's fictions and actually in this life went mournfully about his days somewhere, maybe even in Bangor, Maine, wondering what had happened to his daughter, and whether he might, in this world, have a grandchild he could love. You have to imagine how absolutely Cassie's faith was shaken, and this before she went to knock on the front door of the Burnes house. Reality had become slippery. Facts she thought she'd always known disintegrated, or appeared to. She didn't any longer trust in anything she'd believed to be true; but she was also aware that she might be wrong, that maybe Bev had never lied to her, that her beloved father had in fact died on the highway outside Boston that long-ago night.

Cassie hated Anders Shute and wished powerfully that he had no part in her life. Her mother, in whom she'd long placed her love and sense of safety and of self, loved this man Cassie despised, and seemed prepared to sacrifice her own daughter, her only daughter, for that love. What should Cassie have believed? It was better to think that her mother was crazy, a compulsive liar with terrible judgment, than to believe her mother had dropped Cassie with cause, and had some real reason for her choices. In either case, Cassie was on her own; but in the former, at least, she had hope — for a father, for grandparents, for any of a number of alternative lives, none of which could be worse, she figured, than the one she was living.

Sunday afternoon in Bangor was trickier. She couldn't wander all day through the hospital corridors without attracting suspicion; it wasn't big enough. She figured rightly that the public library would be closed on a Sunday, but she walked there anyway, up from the riverbank to the flat open plaza on Harlow Street. It was hard to blend into the background on a Sunday, she told Peter — not as hard as it would have been in Royston, where everybody really knows everybody, at least by sight — but she still stuck out more than she liked. She felt people were watching her, and once the sun came out and it grew warm, she worried that the beanie over her hair made her particularly noticeable. But the hair — her famous white-blond hair — would have been worse. She kept expecting someone to ask her questions — the blue-rinsed grandma limping out of Rite Aid clutching a prescription bag who glared at her; the little Asian boy who banged his scooter pretty hard into her heel because he wasn't looking; the guy who reminded her of Peter, the same dark curls and gangly arms, about our age, hunched on the library steps tapping on his phone. That was the worst, because she actually wanted his attention, because she was looking at him easily as much as he looked at her, flickering, surreptitious glances unlike the others, a kind of flirting. But he didn't speak, and she didn't either, in the end a good thing, really, if she didn't want to get caught; and she drifted away as breezily as she could to the nearby park, where she sat cross-legged at the foot of a maple, freezing her butt on the cold ground, pretending she was waiting for someone — which, of course, she sort of was. She said to Peter, who repeated it to me, that it was only there — in the park, the prickly packed earth under her and the maple's scaly trunk behind her, its limbs above still winter-bare — that she understood she was a runaway, that she'd put herself in the category of news flashes or Amber Alerts, a minor who wasn't where she was supposed to be.

The craziness of it all dawned on her: why did Anders Shute have any say at all in her fate? How could that be possible? What would it mean to go home, if she ended up going home, or if that was even the right word, by now, for the storybook house in the cul-de-sac with the Encroaching Forest advancing behind it? Where would she ever be at home now, she wondered, and, she told Peter, sitting in that little park she was weighed, as if by a lead mantle, with a great sadness; she could feel her shoulders and her spine collapsing, and even her cheeks grew heavy — the very opposite of the joy she'd experienced that morning under the cherry blossoms. Because it suddenly seemed to her that coming to Bangor had been a terrible, terrible mistake, and that whatever she would find out from Arthur Clarke Burnes, there'd be no coming back from it, no way to unknow it and either she'd be stuck with Bev and Anders with no way out or she'd have lost Bev forever by exposing her as a lifelong liar, and really, honestly, what she wanted was to be able to go back in time, not a long way, just a couple of years, back to the summer before seventh grade, before it all went wrong. To a time of unknowing. (And when Peter told me she'd said that, I was sure that even though she was talking about how things were with Bev, with her mom, that she also meant going back to me, that she wished too that we could have *us* back, that the knot had never been untied.)

When Peter told me this, all that Cassie had said to him that Wednesday afternoon and evening in his bedroom, hidden from his parents and from hers, before she vanished again and none of us knew where, I wanted desperately to believe that I could do something, that I could help to find her, of course, but also that it would matter to her, matter hugely even, that I did, that it was me. Of course, it was her story, what went on up there in Maine, of course it was; it didn't happen to me, even if I feel, now, as though I were there. But if I'm honest, what mattered most to me was how those events affected our story, hers and mine. I wanted her to come back to me. When Peter told me all she'd said, we were in limbo, caught between inhaling and exhaling, and when I tell you what mattered most to me, I'm telling a terrible secret, because all that mattered then to anyone else was simply that we find her.

So what did happen, in the end, in Bangor? Peter wasn't a hundred percent clear about it. Not that Cassie didn't tell him, because she did, but the telling made her upset, and she wasn't particularly lucid. He didn't want to belabor things, to make her go over the story, obviously so painful; for God's sake, he'd figured there'd be time. He figured that even a day or two later, when she'd caught her breath and calmed down, he'd have her repeat the progression of events in such a way that he'd know he'd got it straight. So mostly he let her sob and snivel and swallow her words and leave gaps and double back and not entirely make sense.

As Peter understood it, or as he told it to me: after breakfast with the Swedish girls on Monday morning, using her Google Maps printout from the school library in Royston (a printout that Miss Barrocca wouldn't suggest trying to trace until the following day, and that wouldn't bear fruit until after Cassie had returned to Royston), Cassie walked the two miles to the Burnes house under a light but persistent April drizzle — needly in its persistence. Number 36 Spring Street turned out to be a little bald, in a neighborhood of newish houses with big, unfenced yards and no sidewalks, where a girl standing still in the rain might quickly be noticed; so she didn't pause, on that reconnaissance visit, but walked right by and on for another quarter mile or so before turning and walking back to town. The house looked shabbier in real life than on the computer; maybe it was just the rain, or the end of winter, but the paint was peeling, and the concrete drive crazed like old china. The grass had lost the battle in places to patches of dirt that, in the weather, had dissolved into mud puddles. The house was dark — kids at school, parents at work. Cassie noticed that the basketball hoop over the garage was bent all the way down, as if someone had dangled from it, or tried to, but so that you couldn't shoot a basket, anyway. Later, she remembered that.

When she went back again, the rain had long stopped (though her clothes still felt damp, in spite of the time she spent waving her sweater under the hand dryer in the basement bathroom at the Bangor Library); it was dusk; lights were on in the blue house and in their pooled glow she could see people moving through the rooms — like watching them on TV, she told Peter. But when he told me, I instead was reminded of watching my cousins at Thanksgiving through my own front windows, that strange sense of distance, even where you should belong.

Of course, Cassie didn't belong at that house in that moment. She told Peter that she chickened out then. She couldn't ring the bell, she couldn't even walk up the steps, she stood in the road in the darkening afternoon, peering up into the dioramas of a life that might have been, could have been, maybe should have been hers; until not one but two cars had to swerve slightly to pass her in the dusk, and she retreated.

The Swedish girls had left. The room was

lonely, and Cassie had trouble sleeping. She woke before dawn to return to Spring Street before the day had begun: third time lucky. Tired in every way, tired of the situation and of herself, she wanted to make things happen, to make things clear.

It was barely light when she finally rang the Burneses' bell. Just like the evening before, lights within illuminated the rooms, though differently: a new scene, possibly a new act, in the play. The oldest kid, Jason, answered the door, already in his Catholic school uniform, even a tie. Plumper than in the photos, a bit taller too, he had a mouth like cupid's bow, and that dark down she remembered from the pictures. His lips were a little shiny — bacon, maybe? It smelled like it. She asked to speak to his dad, to Coach Burnes, and the boy looked her up and down — thinking her a kid from the high school, surely? — before he turned and hollered up the stairs.

'Hang on a minute,' he said, neither rudely nor politely. 'If you can just wait here.'

From the house came the jaunty sound of the radio, and piping child voices, water turning on, a knocking pipe. The entrance where Cassie waited, small, was cluttered with boots, scarves, a couple of dropped umbrellas. It smelled of damp. The boy was gone a while, a couple of minutes, and when he clattered down the stairs again he wore a blazer over his shirt and tie, a crest on the pocket.

'He's just coming,' he said, slightly breathless now, and retreated.

Outside, behind her, the sky had grown almost

fully light, a lowering gray day that threatened more rain. Cassie pushed her hands in her jacket pockets, and her shoulders almost to her ears. She told Peter that she tried to slow down her breathing the way we'd been taught in drama class at school, breathing in and out slowly, counting to five at each passage. She figured he took about ten breaths to appear.

Arthur Clarke Burnes was a little guy — or, at least, not a tall guy — but he was solid. His gray tweed jacket pulled tight in the arms and his neck was red. Maybe he'd been freckly; maybe he'd been fair; now he was just ruddy and leathery and mostly bald. His eyes, light blue — like hers, Cassie thought at once — shimmered watery and veined . . . 'rheumy-eyed,' I thought, when Peter told me. They looked, she said to Peter, like maybe he was a drinker, especially with the skin so red. And Coach Burnes looked annoyed. He fumbled with his shirt cuffs, his thick fingers tugging the shirt down inside the unwieldy sleeves.

'Yes?' he said, half-attending. 'Do I know you? What is it?'

Right away, she told Peter, she knew it wasn't what she'd wanted. The timing was off; the emotion wrong. This bullish little man, his fleshy neck spilling over his collar, his thin lips tight. He seemed like he might burst.

'My name is Cassie,' she began. She could hear her voice as if it were someone else's. She could hear her voice trembling, as if on the cusp of tears. 'Cassie Burnes.'

He didn't register her surname; it seemed to

make no impression at all. 'Yeah?'

'I'm not from here,' she went on. 'But I think you know my mother, Bev?'

'Who?'

'Bev. Beverly Burnes. Hospice nurse, Royston, Massachusetts, but formerly of Boston?'

'I don't know a Bev Burnes,' he said, but he looked troubled now, Cassie told Peter, as if something hovered at the edge of his vision.

'About fifteen years ago?'

He frowned.

'I have a photo,' Cassie said, and reached into her backpack for her notebook. In it, she had both a picture of her mother, a couple of years old, and the snapshot of Clarke Burnes in his youth, the one blurry photo.

'What's that?'

'I have a photo, a couple of them.' She fumbled for them. 'Did you ever go by Clarke?'

'Sorry?'

'Did you ever use the name Clarke as your first name?'

'What's this about?'

She held out his photo — she was sure from the expression on his face that it was his photo, that he knew at once where it had been taken, and by whom. Her hands were shaking; the photo fluttered in between them. She was almost certain.

'Where did you get this? What's this about?'

'Art? Arthur, hurry now — your eggs are cold!' His wife's voice, unconcerned, mildly reproachful.

'He's at the door,' the boy called back.

'Student from school.'

'What is this about,' he said, really looking at Cassie now, for the first time, his mouth a grim line, his bulk suddenly menacing.

'I think you know my mom?' She held out the other photo, larger, in better focus, Bev by their mantelpiece, at a party, her cloud of honey hair. 'Or you *knew* her, I guess.'

'I don't know you,' he said. It was like watching a man put on armor in front of you, Cassie told Peter. 'I don't know who you are, or what you're doing here. I don't know what you want. But I think you should go now.'

'Please, will you just look at the photo?'

He glanced, but barely, at Bev. 'Who is this? What is this about? I don't know this person.'

But Cassie told Peter that she could have sworn that he was . . . well, not that he was lying, but that he was *uncertain*. She could have sworn that he got weirder, although of course things were already weird.

His wife's dark head popped around the wall at the top of the stairs. 'Art, it's time now. The kids'll be late.' She didn't look quite the way Cassie had pictured her — in the photos she'd been plump, but her shoulders were thin, almost frail. And she didn't have any accent.

'Coming.' When he turned back to Cassie, Arthur Clarke Burnes held his hand up flat between them, so he couldn't really see her face. Like she was too much to contemplate. He didn't look again at Bev, wavering glossy between them. 'I can't help you,' he said. 'I'm sorry.'

'Look at me,' she told Peter that she told him. 'Look in my eyes — your eyes — and tell me that you don't know who I am.' That was my Cassie, fearless.

He reached around her, carefully, as if she were diseased, she said to Peter, to open the front door. He didn't look at her at all; he averted his watery gaze. Physically, he seemed both as though he might still explode and as though he had already exploded.

'You need to leave now.' His voice was low and tight. 'I am not going to ask again.' He nodded out at the gray morning, a short dip of his skull, his eyes on the pendulous ceiling of cloud.

Cassie walked out the door and he shut it firmly behind her. She heard him slip the deadbolt too. It did not start to rain and she didn't start to cry until she'd walked all the way back into town, and she told Peter that every time a car slid alongside and passed her, she wondered if it was him, Arthur Clarke Burnes, driving his other children into the new day.

* * *

There aren't words for that, for how that felt. I know that, even from afar. She didn't need to say it to Peter — he too could imagine. Cassie was filled with knowledge and uncertainty both, and there was no way back to unknowing. She was certain, in her heart, that this man was her father. She had, all her life, counted on and trusted in her imaginary version of this man. And here he was in the flesh, on this Earth, she said to Peter (or was he? Peter said to me, because neither Peter nor I could muster even a fraction of Cassie's certainty: why would Arthur Clarke Burnes of Bangor, Maine, be her father? Why would her father even be alive, without proof, when he'd been dead all her life?), here he was at last, her guardian angel — except he wasn't, was he, after all? She'd been in love all her life with the doting protector of her dreams. But when she most needed him, when Anders Shute had stolen her mother's love and attention, her father turned out to be real, a man of flesh and blood; and this man had denied her. It was like Peter denying Christ in the Bible, she told Peter. He had looked at her and refused to see her, to acknowledge her existence, even. He had turned his eyes away and closed his door in her face. And when her own mother didn't want her! (Or, Peter said to me, Cassie might well have been inventing it all. Why? I said. And then I answered, for myself, for Cassie, because suddenly I knew: because it seemed to her she had no other choice, no story that both made sense and gave her the possibility of hope.)

Cassie had willed her father into life, and then the man she went to claim, the man she so believed in that she had given him her love long before she stood on his doorstep — that man, not imaginary but real, rejected her utterly. And then nobody wanted her, nobody wanted even to claim her; she had nowhere to go.

But she had, above all, no reason to stay in Bangor, and so she came home. She slept that Tuesday night rough in Boston, having missed the last bus back to Royston; and she showed up at Peter's — at his window, to be precise, after climbing onto the garage roof — on Wednesday afternoon, filthy, frightened, exhausted, and half off her head. Peter thought that was the end, the dénouement; but he was wrong.

Where to go? What next? Who will open the door, and their arms, to me? I know her so well that these thoughts are my own, I can step into her skin, see the world from behind her eyes — our blue eyes that always made us sisters — and I'm grateful, and relieved, that she had the wisdom to choose Peter. Peter is who I would have chosen, if for some reason I felt I couldn't choose me. I wish she'd chosen me. But Peter, he knew what to do, and even though they didn't hang out anymore, he still loved her. He was a protector. She knew better than to head to the Evil Morsel in Portland, which says plenty.

Even so, on Thursday morning when finally she stirred, in a patch of April sunlight, in Peter's room, she found herself alone there with a note from him — '*Pre-cal test, gotta go; can skip Spanish & History; back by 11*' — she knew she couldn't stay. His parents, never especially fond of her — she was not the girlfriend high-key Amy Oundle envisaged for her son, 'destined' as he was — wouldn't take well to her presence in his bed. They wouldn't be the ones to accompany her to her door and to stand at her shoulder as she confronted Bev and Anders Shute. My parents would have done that, or they might have. I would have done that, if she'd asked me.

Instead, she went alone, hopped on the bike

she'd retrieved from behind the Dunkin' Donuts, had chained to a lamppost around the corner from Peter's. How she crossed town unnoticed that morning, not once but twice, she of the flaxen hair that shone so brightly in the daylight — I don't get it. The whole town knew she was missing — or at least half the town did — but this is what I think: you only see what you expect to see. Your brain lets the rest go. Because life's tumult, with its infinite sounds and smells and signs, rushes around you like a river in flood: you can only take in, you can only grasp, so much. And if you've already consigned Cassie to the ranks of the disappeared — all those girls and women snatched by loners or neighbors, battered by fathers, dismembered by jilted lovers, raptured from the bike path or the shopping mall or the late-night bus stop to an invisible and unimagined and nonexistent hereafter — well, if she was already gone, you wouldn't see her, would you? That's what I think.

The house — the cul-de-sac — stood empty in the late morning: Bev's hospice work, the work of Death, waited for no man; and Anders, mercifully for Cassie, was up at the hospital. The Aucoins' bitch barely stirred in the yard as Cassie, a familiar sight, a familiar scent, slipped past. She took a shower; she changed her clothes; she fixed a box of mac and cheese and downed a couple of slices of toast with peanut butter. She left the dirty pot on the stove.

She didn't turn her phone on, not then or later, maybe because the phone had come to seem like an evil portal, the wormhole through which anyone could reach her, when she didn't want to be reached. Aside from Peter — and, I'd like to think, from me, but she wasn't thinking of me — she didn't want to be in contact with anyone just then.

In the two hours before Bev came home, what was Cassie doing? What was she thinking? I say I can slip inside her skin and yes, it's true; I say I knew her better than she knew herself, and yes, it's true; but when I try to go there, in those moments, all I get is a deafening, meaningless blur of sound. She didn't know for sure that Bev would come home first, even if she knew it was likely. She didn't know how Bev would react to finding her runaway daughter returned; but first off, she didn't know how she, Cassie, would react. Don't plan it, don't overthink it, just let it happen, you've got to find a way to bridge the chasm from here to there, from this unthinkable present to some unthinkable future . . . But no, I don't believe there was any thought for the future, not a bit. Betrayed by her mother, denied by her father, she didn't even know what she felt — raw, alone, heartsick, broken, raw — so how could she think? I don't believe there was any thought at all, just sound, the roar, the deafening white noise.

At around two, Bev came home. I only have her version. She didn't plan to stay; she'd forgotten some paperwork pertaining to her 4:30 p.m. home visit, something about the meds. Because it came up again later. I remember that she used the word 'pertaining,' and how weird that was to me. I picture her bustling, her long skirts swirling and her stethoscope draped around her neck, rising and falling on her always breathless bosom — but maybe there's just time for a quick snack? — and suddenly, around the corner, there's Cassie, tiny in her puffy parka (she didn't have her parka when she ran away, did she? Bev thinks), her wet hair hanging limp, perched on a high stool at the kitchen island, cool as you please.

That's not my daughter, Bev said she thought — just for a second she thought it was an imposter, from the look in Cassie's eye. I almost dropped dead, she said, I think I clutched at my heart, it scared the living daylights, her so quiet, like a thief, in the kitchen. Like a thief or a ghost.

Bev, she said, her voice quiet still, and almost menacing, like she was amused: Bev, you're home.

Yes, I am, and so are you, Bev said back. I think I had tears, but it's true, I didn't step around the island and give my girl a hug. I can't explain it. In the moment, I was scared of her, it was like she was an imposter. A changeling. Like they'd given me back a different girl.

Is it, she said. What did that mean? I mean, really?

Is it my home? she said then, low and cold. Bev was angry. Sure I was. What she'd put us through, Anders and me. I'd hardly slept. For days. All over a curfew, can you imagine. Well you might ask, I said, after all your shenanigans. (How well I, Julia, remember that: the word 'shenanigans' pulled from another country, another century — who says shenanigans?) But Cassie wasn't fazed.

I want to ask you about a few things, Bev, she said, with an emphasis on *Bev* that was, Bev later said, frankly sinister. And then, as Bev told it, they weren't questions at all, they were accusations: Bev was a liar, she'd kept Cassie from her father, she'd made up a fake story just so she wouldn't have to confront the terrible truth: she'd been impregnated by a man who'd never loved Bev and didn't want to have a child with her, Cassie was a mistake, she wasn't wanted . . . well, Bev said, you can imagine what it felt like, such wounds inflicted by my own child, the baby girl for whom I've sacrificed *everything*, and then she repeated it for effect: *everything*.

Did I, Julia, did any of us, know whom to believe or what was true? None of us was there, there were no witnesses. So that when Bev then explained that Cassie, in her blue parka already before Bev came in the door, as if she was on the verge, already, of leaving — when Bev explained that Cassie had thwacked the counter and called her mother a fucking lying bitch and then had taken off out the door at a run into the chill spring afternoon (a weak sun pushing through the gray, the forsythia neon in the yard), slinging her backpack onto her shoulders, slamming the front door behind her and leaving *not a trace*, that was the expression Bev used, like something out of a TV show or a detective novel, as in 'vanished without a trace,' a rubric for all the armies of vanished girls and women, inevitably traceless — well, it was tough, in that time, to know what Bev meant, or to know how the scene had really unfolded. It just didn't seem quite right.

Peter and I weren't the only ones to wonder. Even on Thursday there were rumors that the police were suspicious. They spent a long time interviewing not only Bev but also Anders Shute, even though he had an alibi; I mean, he was at work.

My parents, on the face of it, remained reticent and sober. They were trying to be adult, to be calm, trying not to give in to the hysteria that had gripped Royston, already, just a day after Cassie had gone for the second time. They were trying to make me feel there was a precedent for this — one that didn't end with a corpse on a beach or a rattle of bones among the embers of a fire, or a girl with a needle in her arm in a squat down an alley in Boston. My mother said, 'The police are doing their job, is all. They need to know all the people Cassie knows, all the places she might have gone.' And then, 'Are you sure, sweetie, she didn't send you a text? Nothing? To your friend Peter, even?'

'She closed it all down, Mom. She turned it all off, days ago. She doesn't want to be found.'

Peter told the police what he knew. Someone said they'd seen a girl in a blue parka getting into a car on Route 29, on the shoulder, about half a mile north of the Burneses' place, at about the right time. The car, white or silver they thought, a sedan.

By Friday morning, Cassie's photo was up on

the LED billboard near the Lotus Garden, smirking down at every driver and every passenger on Route 29, and the police as far as Boston were on the lookout for a near-albino runaway, 5′3″ and 104 pounds (she wouldn't want her weight out there, I knew), wearing a sky-blue puffer, the thin-tube kind, skinny jeans, and a pair of black Nikes on her feet. The official description said nothing about the gap between her teeth, or the lopsidedness of her smile, and I couldn't help but think that she'd have changed her coat and dyed her hair by the time they issued the description — it was pretty basic, wasn't it? Even I would know to do that.

Had Bev really let her daughter, her one and only precious, beautiful daughter, run out the front door when only just retrieved from the abyss, almost returned from the dead, without trying, at least, to stop her? Why hadn't she pursued her, driven up the road even a few minutes later? There had to have been a considerable lag between the moment Cassie bolted and when she climbed into the front passenger seat of the light-colored sedan, not three minutes but more like ten or fifteen, and how could it be that her mother, in those minutes, did absolutely nothing to save her?

By Friday we heard of sightings reported everywhere — in Haverhill, of course, in Newburyport, but in Portsmouth too, at Faneuil Hall in Boston, even in Provincetown, although nobody I knew believed in that one. At school, everyone had their own ideas. I kept expecting someone to ask me what I knew, because I knew

Cassie better than anybody; but Peter was the only one. It didn't occur to people that I'd have anything to say, because our friendship had been 'over' since the beginning of middle school. Two years — two and a half, maybe — but it wasn't like we didn't speak at all. Never mind that we'd been conjoined all our lives, Siamese twins until the Evil Morsel. Never mind that we were sisters under the skin. But Peter understood. He sought me out and told me all he knew, and all he'd told the detective. He told me what her friends were saying — they thought she'd made a beeline to New York, that was *so obvious*. They said she'd talked about being a model there — this was Mason, Cassie's friend for all of six months, dumb but gorgeous, in a rotating collection of Lululemon from the outlet mall up in Kittery — and that Brianna's cousin Jae might have heard from her, even: he'd had calls from a Massachusetts cell number that he'd thought at first were random, but it might have been her, right? Another of her friends, Alma, the girl she'd got in trouble for, thought she might be on her way to Florida — spring break still down there, if she'd hitched all the way, and then if you just hooked up with the right guy, you could be set for a long time.

Luckily I didn't have to hear these girls spout this idiotic stuff. They told Peter, ever-patient ally or frank double-agent, and Peter repeated it to me, and that Thursday afternoon we walked out of school and sat on the climbing structure in the playground down the road — the playground they'd been rebuilding that long-ago summer when Cassie hurt her hand at the animal shelter. A raw breeze insinuated itself under our jackets, the kind that makes you turn your collar up, and the metal platform froze my butt through my cords. Peter wasn't wearing a proper jacket, just a sweatshirt — colby on it in big white letters — and he bunched his fists underneath it against his belly for warmth, so he looked pregnant. Another time, I might have made a joke about it.

'You don't think she's in Florida or New York City,' I said.

He shook his head. We pushed our backs against the bright metal poles of the structure, up high, our legs tucked up in front of us. We could see out through the trees — branches, mostly, their imminent leaves still tight buds — to the road, where occasional cars swished mournfully by. I felt as though we were in a story about ourselves, the story that was, at last, adult life; and I didn't want to be there. We sat in silence for a minute; I pulled on a thread at my knee, the edge of the hole in my professionally holey jeans, the ones I'd promised my mother I wouldn't wear to school.

'You don't think — ' I said.

And then I stopped. I couldn't say what I thought we were both thinking.

'A lot of shit can go wrong in this world,' Peter said. 'But we don't have any evidence that anything has. Right?'

'I guess.'

'No, that's the truth. All we know is that we don't know.'

'That doesn't help much.'

'You've gotta start somewhere,' he said. I looked at his hands, his long fingers with their clean, square nails. Sometimes I still couldn't believe he didn't desire me back. Even then, there, I could anticipate his every movement, as if he were surrounded by a force-field, so compelling it almost repelled. Surely he was aware of it? But was he not saying: all we know is that we don't know; and if this was true about Cassie, was it not also true about everything, every uncertain action to which we attribute such certainty?

'Look,' he said, the tip of his bony nose and the rims of his nostrils reddening in the cold, 'until she showed up in my room — literally in my room — on Tuesday, we thought she might be dead, right? Until she just appeared, it seemed like she'd fallen off the planet.'

'True.'

'We didn't know whether to believe what Bev and Shute were saying had happened. You can't say we didn't wonder if she was under a pile of leaves in the woods behind their house.'

'In the Encroaching Forest,' I said, though only Cassie would have understood. I tore at the skin on my lip with my front teeth until I tasted blood. How important it had been in those few days not to allow that thought — that image — not to articulate it to Peter or my parents, and not to myself. But it was true: you couldn't say we hadn't wondered, looking at Shute's eyes and thin lips, at the grimace of supposed anguish that could easily have been a smirk; and at Bev, whose abundant flesh had always made her seem jolly but who now seemed potentially dark.

'She wasn't in danger then,' Peter said, 'so why should she be in danger now?'

'Because before, she left a note, and took her bike.'

'But this time she took her coat.' We lapsed again into silence.

'Do you think she knew where she was going?'

Peter shook his head slightly, looking out through the trees. 'She's not in a good way,' he said. 'This whole Clarke Burnes thing has messed with her head.'

'This whole Anders Shute thing,' I said, 'or Bev thing.'

'This whole life thing.'

I closed my eyes. You could hear, muffled, the gentle cars, and far off the shouts and laughter of the kids in the yard at the high school. There was nobody in the kiddie playground but us, teenagers way too big for it, and the air smelled of wet earth and cold metal. For a second I thought that maybe when I opened my eyes, she'd be there, rocking on the springed purple pony down below, knees to her chin, smiling wide. But I realized that Cassie in my mind's eye wasn't the girl of now but the girl of then, pure figment, gone.

Just then, Nancy, our egret, that unlikely vision that Cassie and I had named the summer before everything changed — or maybe it was Nancy's cousin — came to remind me of the quarry. There wasn't any logic to it, not when Cassie had last been seen getting into a car on the highway. If she was looking to fly, it wouldn't be a flight away but a flight back, almost time travel. But it was the strangest thing, in April, in Massachusetts, in the barely relieved damp of early spring, to see behind Peter's shoulder, in the distance, the slow, prehistoric ascent of an egret from the half-empty, leaf-sodden ornamental pond at the park's far end. The waving of those thin, dark, vast wings bothered my peripheral vision and I turned, at speed — was it a ghost? I wondered fleetingly — to see her deliberate, inexorable rise, that *S*-bend neck tucked, the webby feet retracting like an airplane's wheels. And I thought, It's April — I can't be seeing this: Nancy, in Royston, now, and I reached without thinking to grab Peter's arm — I could tell he was surprised; he flinched a little, or his forearm did, beneath my hand; because we didn't touch much, Peter and I, by which I mean, we never touched, an awkwardness I could interpret in various ways, both flattering and unflattering, and which I had chosen for a long while simply not to think about. 'Look,' I whispered. 'Nancy.'

'Who's Nancy?' I could hear in his voice that he was smiling, but I didn't look at him, because I couldn't look away from the bird, black and graceful and awkward against the ominous sky. I pointed, and could hear Peter's intake of breath. 'What's she doing here?' he asked. 'Wrong season, right?'

'It's like she isn't even real,' I said, by which time she was gone into the tree shadows beyond the park.

'Who's Nancy then?' Peter asked after a minute, standing and swinging himself down the pole to the ground. 'My butt is freezing.'

'Yeah. It's still cold.' I slid down the slide instead. When I put my hands on my rear end I could feel the refrigerated flesh through my jeans. I explained to Peter about Nancy, about the inside joke she'd been between Cassie and me in our last twinned summer, when we could never have imagined coming unstuck, and expected to be friends always.

'I haven't seen a Nancy bird in a long time. Like, maybe she sent her.'

'Never say never, I guess. Which leads you to what, exactly? What's the message, if there is one?'

I said that we should go to the quarry.

'You're kidding, right?' he pointed at the sky. 'This weather? And it's five o'clock already. What are you hoping to find? Why in God's name would she go there? Like, she's made a Girl Scout tent out of broken fir branches and is building a fire to roast fiddleheads?'

'Like, maybe,' I said. Ordinarily, I might have worried that Peter would laugh at me, but finding Cassie was the most important thing. 'Trust me,' I said, and all but involuntarily I touched his arm again. It wasn't flirting, it was urgency, and he understood this. He didn't flinch that time.

The walk took longer than I remembered. Neither of us spoke much. The late sun tried without success to break through the woolly gray, the soft gravel shoulder beneath our feet was still sodden, and, once we passed the Barkers' house, the endless wall of evergreens pressed mournful and darkly moist alongside us. The turn-off to the quarry was overgrown after the winter months' disuse, and the undergrowth seemed to hover between last winter's death and spring's coming life, a combination of slimy leaf piles and tightly nubbed boughs, on their surfaces juicy green buttons ready to burst. The rutted dirt path dissolved in places into puddles, but the way ahead was clear. The parking lot lay empty, of course. Just the occasional scurrying squirrel; an early bird or two, rustling and chirruping. The quarry was silent, its surface black and glassy.

'You're joking, J, right?' Peter's chin tucked into the neck of his sweatshirt. His red nostrils glistened.

'It's just a feeling. Let's walk the perimeter, okay? Just in case?'

'The roaring fiddlehead fire, right?'

'Or something.'

'A bird is not a sign, you know.'

'How can we be sure?'

Peter, irritated, rolled mucus in his throat; but he didn't walk away. We couldn't afford not to look. We set off together around the quarry. The path proved more treacherous than I expected. There was no straightforward circuit around the water's edge; the glinting rocks were slick underfoot and the bushes wild, their thorny fingers clawing at our necks and wrists.

'What are we looking for exactly?' Peter asked, arms akimbo on a high outcrop over the still water, as far from the parking lot as we could be. His breath made smoky whorls in the chill. 'Because this feels as futile as anything I've ever done.'

I couldn't contradict him. 'I thought there'd be some trace of her. I thought she might have come here.'

'Because?'

I shrugged. I couldn't say because it was a place that mattered to us, to her and me; because when we were here, we were happy, and happy together, and had homes and parents and believed we always would. That wasn't a reason for anything.

'Julia,' Peter touched me this time, his hand on my shoulder. His voice was low and almost harsh. 'You think she might be here because this is where *you* lost her. But it's a long time ago.' Then he let go of me, and turned away.

Even so, as we picked our way back to the start, I kept my eyes open for the first flutter of a ribbon, or the glimmer of an earring on the forest floor. I peered for footprints in the squelchy mud — little feet; recent prints — or a cell phone, or a house key, or a shiny dime. Hansel and Gretel; *Scooby-Doo; Tintin in Tibet; Picnic at Hanging Rock;* always, always, there was a sign. Of Cassie, at the quarry, there was no sign.

Peter walked me home — it was past dusk by then, and I was late for supper — and he then called his mother to come pick him up. With my parents, he was strained — both superpolite and awkward — and although the obvious reason was that he was holding up our meal, I figured he didn't want them to get the wrong idea, to think that there was anything between us. He stayed standing in the front hall — 'My mom's just on her way' — and made stilted, bright conversation about the track team and how he dreamed of going to UPenn one day, if he could get in. His mother had gone there. We didn't mention Cassie, but she stood in the front hall with us. When his mother pulled up, she honked from the street and he darted out the door. 'Sorry to have kept you from your dinner,' he said to my parents. 'We shouldn't have lost track of time.' And to me, without looking back, 'See you in school.'

I raised a hand, a sort of wave, but he wouldn't have seen. Over dinner, my mother asked if there'd been any announcements about Cassie at school. My father said that one of his patients, Rose Bremner, said she'd heard on the police scanner that they had some leads up near Newburyport. I nodded and shifted my mashed potatoes around on the plate, flattening them with my fork. A lot of time had gone by now; she could be anywhere. She could even be back in Bangor, although I assumed the police had already thought to look there. We didn't talk about it, about her, very long. There wasn't much to say. My mother asked about speech team, what I was preparing for the next tournament. I sensed she wanted to ask me about Peter — she knew I still liked him — but she didn't.

After dinner, when the dishes were done and I

was heading upstairs, she came and put her arms around me and held me to her. Then she pulled back and stroked my cheek, tucked my hair behind my ear. Her eyes were sad. She didn't say anything. She didn't need to.

* * *

I woke before dawn. Although the air in my bedroom was cold, I was sweating under the covers. Saturday morning: no call to get up. But my heart was on alert, my dream still with me in the room. Cassie: of course. As she was, yes, but not with the sense that this was the past. It was now. We were playing a game, the kind of pretend game that we'd played for years: You be the monster, I'll be the knight. You be the pilot, I'll be the Resistance fighter. You be the fugitive, and I'll find you. You be the dark wizard, and I'll be the centurion of light. You be the returned soldier, I'll be your wife. In the dream, Cassie, with her white-blond hair, put on a black feathered cloak — a bird cloak, a Nancy cloak — that promised to hide her, fugitive, wizard, teenage girl, and to enable her to fly. Only, within seconds, it burned into her skin, grafted itself, became exquisitely, agonizingly, irremovable. Hers was poisoned, a poisoned cloak. She shrieked in pain, her eyes white-edged, bulging, her arms reaching for me. And there was nothing I could do but stand there and watch, a reluctant but unwavering witness. Her shrieks woke me into the frigid dark, but I couldn't figure out to what waking sound they might correspond — a bat? A cat in heat? And even with my eyes open, I could still see her, my Cassie, enveloped in the fronded, feathery blackness, all but her white head and hands, withering under the dark mantle.

Where was she? Where were we playing? What was our ill-fated game? I knew it, I could smell it, the site hovered on the cusp of my consciousness, just out of reach. I closed my eyes again, listened to the way her voice echoed, reverberating off the walls. In the darkness behind my lids, I saw the glimmering fragments of stained glass, and felt the smooth heft of the banister under my hand. I looked up. And then I realized what I had to do, in the early spring predawn darkness. Worried, of course, I was suddenly certain too, precisely because this wasn't a kids' game or an imaginary scenario, because with every minute the cloak burned further into Cassie's flesh, and if I didn't hurry, she would never fly, she wouldn't even survive. There would be no way ever to get it off.

I only fleetingly considered waking my parents. They wouldn't have understood: like Peter, they would have thought I was making things up. 'You have an overactive imagination,' my mother liked to say. I needed an ally who believed the way I did in premonitions and auguries, in instincts rather than logic. Like a kid, or a prophet — or like a Hagrid. It took me only a minute to recall Bessie and the derecho; and that too came to me not as a thought but like something I knew in my deepest self, like in a dream. I looked up the number I still had in my contacts from when I did my speech team monologue in seventh grade, and even though I could see all too clearly that the clock's green light read 4:43 a.m., I called Rudy Molinaro.

Did I waken him? Hard to say. Was he surprised? I'd guess so, extremely even; but he's not a man of many words, nor one to show emotion. Flat affect, my mother would call it.

I told him it was about the little blond girl. The angel, I reminded him. Her name is Cassie, I said. She needs me, I said. She needs our help. As I spoke to him, I could picture those jelly-bean eyes shining dully in their pouchy sockets. It was still night, early on a Saturday morning. I was a kid calling him — less than half his age. But he listened to me, and reacted as if I were the mayor of Royston, as if it were perfectly understood that if I asked him to do something so unusual, it was only because it *simply needed to be done*. Because it was essential.

Would my parents, would Peter, have accused Rudy of being a stupid guy (not the *brightest light*, not the *sharpest knife*)? Sure. But that morning I was grateful, because I needed someone who could help me, who wouldn't tell me I was just a kid, or irrational, or wrong before we even set out. He knew how important feelings were, having a sense or an intuition for something. He was the guy who trusted his dog Bessie over everyone else.

Was he drunk? I would have said, when speaking to him, probably. Once I got into his truck, I could have told you with absolute certainty, yes. Even with Bessie panting her hot dog breath between us in the front seat, I was bathed in the reek of him, cigarettes and booze fumes, like he sweated it out through his pores. I didn't mind. That probably helped me out a bit, that he was drunk that way; it made our dreamlike journey seem even less real, like he was dreaming it too.

I wasn't afraid, to get into Rudy Molinaro's truck at 5:20 on a Saturday morning in April, still in the dark, nobody knowing what we were doing or where we were going. I wasn't one bit afraid. All I can say is that I trusted him, drunk and lonely as he was. Because of Bessie, I trusted him; because of all the time and love he'd given to his sick mother. Because he was the opposite of cruel, and he didn't really know how to think of what he wanted. It didn't occur to me until much later, after it was all in the past, that in those hours I could have been — in some other circumstance, I could well have been — terrified.

We didn't say much, in the fug of the cabin, on the ride over to the asylum, vents blaring hot air, Bessie's panting our version of dialogue. Rudy was kind of panting too, or at least breathing noisily, as though every airway that could be stuffed up, was. His face shone in the reflected dashboard lights, almost clay-colored. I too breathed through my mouth, on account of the smells.

'It's a good idea to look, I figure,' he said eventually, after chewing a while on his cheek. Bessie licked her lips as if in agreement and yawned, making a squeak in her throat like an unoiled hinge. Her teeth loomed close to my ear.

'Just seems that way,' I agreed. My hands were clasped in my lap, as if I were in church. And then, except for the vents and the breathing and the sound of Bessie maneuvering her saliva, we fell quiet again.

Rudy got down from the truck to unlock the giant padlock on the main gate at the road. I don't know what I'd thought — that we would bushwhack in from the quarry in the twilight? — but I hadn't pictured us arriving along the central driveway. The truck bucked and rolled, even at ten miles an hour, branches scraping and snapping at our sides. No vehicle had traveled this way in a long while. The headlamps jounced crazily, illuminating now a hummock of dirt, now the broken path ahead, now a tangle of trees. The Bonnybrook rose suddenly before us, around a bend in the track, its haggard hulk black against the bruise-blue, just-leavening sky.

From outside, it didn't appear that anything had changed in the years since Cassie and I had been there — the much-debated construction projects had apparently never broken ground, had remained imaginary. But that didn't mean that nobody had set foot there, or that time hadn't further ravaged the ruins. From a distance, it looked as though more windows were broken, more shutters missing or dangling. More graffiti spread along the walls. When Rudy turned off the truck, his headlights stayed on, blaring at the chained main entrance that Cassie and I had bypassed long ago. Rudy reached across in front of me and took a large silver flashlight out of the glove compartment. I could almost feel its weight in his hand. He grunted as he hopped down to the ground. Bessie flew over him, landed weightlessly. She sniffed the air, ears pricked; and decided not to bark. Whatever rustled in the bushes was beneath her notice. I wished I knew her well enough to embrace her rusty scruff, to throw myself at her mercy.

Rudy waved the torchlight around the Bonnybrook's face, the effect that of a spotlight in a disco. 'Where'd you say you went in?'

'I'm not sure that I said.' I led him toward the dining-room windows.

'It's trespassing, you know.' He said this without apparent judgment, a simple observation. 'It's against the law.'

'We were just kids,' I said.

He grunted, and paused to rub an eye. 'But you knew that,' he insisted.

'I guess we did.'

* * *

The French window we'd gone through, more decrepit than it had been, was barely there at all; just a frame. Rain had destroyed the parquet floor inside, and it buckled like waves in a small harbor. Broken glass glinted everywhere underfoot. The room felt different, somehow: I realized, as Rudy shone his light from side to side, that everything that could be removed — anything moveable — was gone. There was nothing in the room but itself. Even the wagon-wheel light fixtures had been yanked from the ceiling, leaving behind broken plaster and dangling wires.

'Where to?' Rudy knocked his head from side to side as if it was a pointer. 'Which way?'

'I think upstairs. I'm sorry.'

The Bonnybrook made its own songs, creaks and pops and a series of high-pitched whines as the wind passed through it. Outside, the day's light began to bleed over the horizon, but in the asylum's front hall you wouldn't have known: without Rudy's flashlight, we would have been in blackness. He shone it jerkily around us: dust motes drifted in the air; the rutted floor had been stripped of its boards by salvagers; the balustrade itself, the flowered stained-glass window — all had vanished. There were no longer any glamorous ghosts; even the ghosts had fled. All that was left was the cold smell of damp, as of the earth reclaiming its territory. The stairs rose skeletal before us into the darkness.

Bessie, apparently unruffled, whined slightly and started climbing.

'All right, girl. If you say so.' The air around us hung as thick as matter. I was so grateful for Rudy's presence, in his minor cloud of booze and tobacco stink, that I put my fingertips to the back of his down coat, just lightly, so we were connected as we climbed.

⋆ ⋆ ⋆

I had known in my marrow that she would be there. I had known from the moment I woke up. Maybe I had known from the moment I saw

Nancy. Cassie was my best friend; we made each other. Bessie found her within a couple of minutes — Bessie, who took off at a trot as soon as we reached the second story, not waiting for us trepidatious humans, not looking back. We could hear her toenails clatter along the floor, and the rhythmic thud of her too. We could sense her digressions, into one room, a circuit, into the next, the hollow jangling of her tags. We followed slowly, Rudy waving his torch in the gloom, though he didn't need it by then.

'She'll be here, Rudy,' I said. 'You'll see.'

His grunt was noncommittal. The day was dawning, gray-blue, seeping now even into the dark inner hallway, cold shafts of low light. This seemed suddenly less surreal, and less real too. In what childish fit of insanity had I orchestrated this? As if it were all a game or a story, as if she would do as I imagined her — as I willed her — to have done?

But then Bessie barked, down in the darkest subcorridor of what Cassie and I had named the Isolation Ward. Rudy broke into what was, for him I guess, a run, a sort of lumbering wheezy haste, and I ran on ahead of him, able now at least to see dark spots in the flooring and avoid twisting my ankle.

Room 7, one with no gold or crimson blooms of mold on the walls, and with, still, a blackened sink, dry as dust. Our room. Chicken-wire glass at the high windows; a metal door half off its hinges, as if someone had thought to steal it, and renounced. Bessie stood guard over a blue down form curled against one wall, a ski-jacket blob with stick limbs and a limp tangle of white-blond hair. Bessie alternately stamped her paws excitedly, wagging her tail and barking, and ran forward to try to lick — literally lick — Cassie into shape. Cassie, neither fully conscious nor unconscious, had battened her arms over her face. She writhed and moaned — 'No, no, no,' was all I got — more intensely when Bessie's tongue slurped at her. 'No, no, no.'

I took in the plastic jug of Smirnoff, largely empty, and the yellow Wheat Thins box knocked on its side, its wax bag half spilled out. A two-liter Diet Coke bottle, lid off, half full. There was her backpack too, almost empty, a deflated sack, and next to it, a couple of orange prescription pill bottles, their big white caps bright wheels on the dirty tiles. I stood in the doorway, just looking, as Rudy huffed up behind me. I didn't say anything.

'No, no, no,' Cassie moaned.

'Fuck me,' Rudy breathed in my ear, like he'd thought it was all a story too, and now couldn't believe what he saw. But Bessie, although not entirely calm (she was justifiably excited; she'd won the game) knew that the prize was human and the consequences real. Once Rudy stood beside me, Bessie stopped barking: still stamping and wagging, she turned her head to look at Rudy, then back at Cassie, then back to Rudy again. He was clearly supposed to tell her what to do next.

'Good girl, Bessie,' he managed; and 'Sit,' which, tremblingly, she did. 'Fuck me. Fuck me,' he kept whispering. He handed me the flashlight, which I turned off — excessive now. We didn't need it to see Cassie lying there in the corner. He fumbled for his cell phone, and punched the number.

Only slowly did I become aware of the reek around us, of vomit and the other too. A sort of olfactory complement to Rudy's, in a way. Cassie wasn't dead by any means; but not for want of trying.

Rudy, wincing from the stench, stepped forward and tried gently to rouse her, tenderly shaking her shoulder. Another muffled rebuff. She wouldn't lift her arms away from her face. I imagined her eyes were closed, but we couldn't tell. Her famous hair lay snarled around her in the dust. My back against the wall, as far from her as I could be and still be in the room, I slid to the floor and waited, my knees to my chest. Lord, it was cold in that room — even though there was still glass at the window. I noticed that: she'd chosen a room where the window was still shut, where the wind could be kept out. I didn't say a thing. When Rudy and Bessie left to go meet the medics down at the driveway, I didn't move. It was full daylight by then. I watched her down jacket rise and fall with her breath. She snored a little. As far as I knew, she didn't even know I was there.

The ambulance men finally appeared, a ruckus in the stairwell and along the corridor, all clanking stretcher and jaunty banter, and I thought then she would stir; but even though they spoke to her directly and asked her questions, she didn't speak.

'She's awake all right,' the bearded one observed, pulling unsuccessfully at the arm clamped across her head. 'She may not want to be, but she is.'

'What a fucking mess,' said the other one. And, to me, 'Give us a hand and pack up this shit?' He gestured to the bottles and the bag.

'You're the friend, eh?' asked the bearded one as I knelt down to follow instructions, putting the pill bottles and the crackers into the backpack, casting around for the lid to the Coke bottle.

'That's right,' said Rudy from the doorway, where he stood smoking a cigarette, perhaps to mask the smell. 'If not for this one, we'd be none the wiser. Police thought she was gone to New York, or up north, or something.'

The surly medic shook his head, intent on strapping Cassie, now willfully rigid all over, to the stretcher. 'Fucking mess,' he said again.

'Good for you.' The other guy tilted his head at me. 'You probably saved her life.'

But then there was a moment, while they fussed around her body, while Rudy, exhausted, smoked with his eyes all but closed and stroked Bessie's now-quiet head, scratching her gently behind the ears, a moment when I was alone in watching Cassie properly — her head I mean. She moved the defending arms, just slightly, so that I could glimpse her eyes glittering behind them, as if from within a cave: open, alert, they turned on me with a rage I hadn't known in all our years, a rage essentially murderous. I could swear her lips moved, that she spoke to me

— silently, I mean, she mouthed the words, just three of them: *Fuck you, traitor*. I could swear that's what she said.

* * *

By mid-June, they were gone. When ninth grade drew to a close, so too did the familiar shape of my life up to that point: whatever lay ahead, I had to accept that my friendship with Cassie — my defining friendship — was truly finished. Through that first summer and fall, I clung to Peter and he to me: Cassie did, in that sense, give me what I wanted. I got to have Peter as my boyfriend for over six months, six whole months in which we reassured ourselves that each of us had acted for the best, for Cassie's best; and that we were the only two — obviously — who had truly known and understood her.

But it's a strange thing, to share your love with a phantom — or more than that, to feel that the love between you is basically love destined for her that she threw back at you. How else could we have gone in a matter of a few weeks from Peter recoiling when I touched him to his not being able to keep his hands off me? Jodie said it was all perfectly logical, that he'd pulled back in the first place because of how much he desired me, but that he'd felt it would be wrong on account of Cassie, especially when she was in trouble, and so on. Her version was the inverse of mine, like the Escher drawing of a staircase in our attic bathroom; but I could only see things her way intermittently, and I kept worrying that when he kissed me and closed his eyes, he saw Cassie, or that when he slipped his hand onto my leg at the movies or when we watched TV, he was comparing, in his mind, the doll-like breadth of Cassie's thigh beneath his palm, and the substantial weight of mine. When we talked about poetry or played music, I didn't worry; those passions we shared weren't hers. But then he wrote another song about her — another ballad, with a sweet refrain about how she smelled of roses — and then that too was tainted.

So maybe I killed things because I was so sure they were dying — like everything else, like all my stories it sometimes seems, I willed the make-believe into reality, fiction into fact, as if imagining made it so. Or maybe I was right all along. By Christmas, anyway, we agreed we were better off as friends — it made us seem like characters in a novel, and certainly it was coolest to stay close to your exes, in that nonchalant but affectionate way where the next girlfriend couldn't worry, but also couldn't help but worry. Above all, I didn't want to be the sad girl, the one who lost her girlfriend not once but twice, and then lost in love in the bargain; although like the Escher drawing, once you've seen things from a certain perspective, you can't entirely unsee them.

My story about Peter and me worked out pretty well; we really were good friends, almost inseparable friends, until late in the spring of tenth grade — eleventh for him — when Peter started seeing Djamila, a new girl in his year with green eyes and fine café-au-lait skin and a beautiful — really beautiful — spirit. She was in eleventh grade too at that point, and she ran track too, and she sang, in the bargain. Everyone really liked her — *I* really liked her — and when she opened her mouth, it was like Whitney Houston suddenly appeared in the room.

But all that is much later. I'm still here. I'm fine. I'll be a senior soon. I still go once a week to see a therapist in Newburyport that the school shrink recommended to my parents. My mother drives me and waits in the local Dunkin' Donuts with her laptop while I sit in the woman's drab office, overlooking a parking lot. It has a daybed, which I ignore, and a hard chair, on which I sit, and a large potted fern. Boxes of Kleenex strategically dotted around.

On the wall hangs a strange dark painting, a sort of fairy scene of sprites and toadstools in a night forest. Why? Who would choose that, whimsical but super dark? One of the sprites — with hideously shimmery wings like a dragonfly — has white-blond hair and reminds me of Cassie. More than that, the sprite reminds me of my dream about Cassie and her black feathered flying cloak, the poisoned cloak that would kill her instead of setting her free. Every week when I look at that painting, it is like a goad, urging me to tell this woman about that dream, about that girl, about what I now know — not in words, but just in knowledge, like a weight in the atmosphere, like the residue of an odor — about growing up. Each week, I resolve more firmly to say nothing about it.

Now I know, for what little it's worth, what it means to be a girl growing up. Maybe you can choose not to put on the cloak, but then you'll never be free, you can never soar. Or you can take on the mantle that is given you; but what the consequences may be, what the mantle might do, what wearing it may entail, you can't know beforehand. Others may see better, but they can't save you. All any of us can do for another person is to have the courage not to turn away. I didn't, until I did.

We have little to say to each other, this therapist and I. She's a nice lady, but honestly, what does she know? To her, I'm another mildly troubled teen, a girl whose friend got really depressed. But my curse is to *see* things, to know stories, how they unfold, and people, what they are like. I don't seek to know these things, I just do. It tires me, to be honest. Cassie got the prophetic name, but I got the curse — or the gift, depending how you look at it. If the nice lady saw these things too, then there'd be no need to explain; but if she doesn't — and at this point, I'd venture with some confidence that she doesn't — then there's no point in trying. What I'd like is for someone to take the burden from me, or at least to share it. If I didn't see, I wouldn't try to know; and of course, you can't ever really know what happens to another person, or what they think happens to them, which amounts to the same thing. I can't know what the poisoned cloak felt like burning into Cassie's skin. I can't even really imagine it.

* * *

After the ambulance men left to ferry Cassie up to Haverhill, and the policeman came to take charge of her stuff, Rudy took me home. My parents hadn't woken up yet, so they might never have known I'd been gone. Rudy wasn't the kind of grown-up to march me to the front door and engage my mother in conversation — he was probably more afraid of my parents than were most of my friends. We sat for a few minutes in the warm cab of his truck, the three of us — him, Bessie, me — hollowed out by the morning's events. The stink wasn't as strong by then, or maybe my nose had just been filled up.

'Rudy,' I said eventually, 'thank you. And Bessie — ' She turned a hooded eye in my direction, and sleepily bared a fang.

'Paramedic seems to think she'll be okay.' Rudy's grubby hands clutched the steering wheel with force.

'I'd better go in. My parents will be wondering where I am.'

'Sure thing, missy.' I thought he might lean toward me, across the dog, but he didn't. 'When you go visit her, tell her Rudy's glad she's okay, okay?'

As I slipped into the house, I thought that Rudy had never once asked why I thought Cassie would be at the Bonnybrook. He trusted that I knew. I wondered whether my parents would be angry with me when I told them what we'd done. I'd have to tell them about my time there with Cassie, years before; my mother especially wouldn't be pleased.

I was right. I could see my mother's face darken when I recounted the history, as if she looked at her daughter and realized I wasn't the kid she'd always believed me to be. She didn't say anything in particular, nodded, but I could tell that the story of me and Cassie playing at the asylum that long-ago summer unsettled her almost as much as Cassie's current story. On some level, in some unsayable way, my mother didn't care that much about Cassie anymore. She was relieved that Cassie had been found, and was safe, but beyond that, she didn't need to know. *I* was what mattered to her; and when, for so many years, Cassie had been a part of me, she had been important to my mother. But my mother had written Cassie off, long before. To my parents, she was what's commonly called 'bad news,' the sort of kid for whom muted pity is the most optimistic possible response.

This wasn't only true of my mother. It was just the truth of it. On Monday, in school, the principal gathered an allschool assembly in the gym to announce that Cassie had been found and was in stable condition in the hospital, and in the loving care of her family, so we could all rejoice; he used the word 'rejoice,' peculiar to me. He loomed at the podium, thick-thighed in his tight suit with his careful coif, looking like an aging rocker at a wedding, and he said, would we all please give Cassie and her family (her family? Anders Shute?) their privacy, at which comment I could hear some enraging titters behind me in the crowd; and then he said this was a personal matter only, we did not have any reason to discuss it further, so please not to speculate or spread rumors. Then he dismissed us to our classrooms, and of course in the hallways nobody spoke of anything but Cassie.

'Hey, Julia.' A tenth grader named Ollie who had never spoken to me before sidled up close. 'We hear you were in on it, helped her hide out.'

I didn't reply, kept going, looked at the ground.

'Don't believe everything you hear,' Jodie said for me.

'That girl was a slut,' one of Ollie's friends offered. 'Don't you remember last fall at AJ's party? She was totally wasted.'

'And I suppose you weren't, fuckboy?' I was surprised, because I knew Jodie thought Cassie was a slut too. But Jodie hated the boys' hypocrisy most of all.

'Well, I don't know,' the guy kept pushing, 'I didn't end up half-naked in a room with a bunch of girls, did I?'

'Only in your dreams,' Jodie replied, pulling me away by the elbow.

'Call your mom,' she suggested. 'Head home. Take the day, and maybe tomorrow. This will quiet down.'

'It might not.'

'Believe me, it will.'

'Why are you so sure?'

'Because,' Jodie said, 'it's like before, when you kept thinking Cassie was cool. You can't see the truth because you care too much about her. It distorts your vision. The truth is, she was way more interesting to people when she was missing. Now they know the ending to the story. It's over. And the ending isn't as exciting as everything they'd imagined: she could have been a teenage prostitute in Times Square. She could have found a sugar daddy in Florida. She could have been abducted. She could have been murdered and chopped up and bits of her scattered along the beach at Plum Island. Any of those things would have made her special, and remembered. Someone might have made a movie about her, or put her on the news. There might have been a trial. But it turns out she's just another kid who had a huge blow-up with her mom, and went to sleep a couple of nights in an abandoned building.'

'She stole drugs from her mom's medical kit. She tried to kill herself.'

'Okay, she gets a couple of interest points for that; but nobody at school knows that yet. And it would've made a better story if she'd actually succeeded.'

'Wow. Harsh.'

'Think of it as a speech team story, if you had to write it up. The happy ending is no ending. Nobody particularly wants the happy ending when they care more about the story than the person.'

'How can you be so mean?'

'I'm not being mean,' Jodie said. 'I'm just telling it like it is.'

I went home that day and I took off the next day, the Tuesday, and went back to school on Wednesday. A few people seemed to look at me and whisper, as if saying *Yeah, she's the friend who found her*; and Cassie's new friends, Alma and a girl called Justine, sought me out in the cafeteria and asked me what had happened. I didn't tell them the details — not about the vomit, or the vodka, or the pill bottles — I just told them she'd gone to hide out in the asylum and I'd guessed she might be there because of when we were younger. I heard through the grapevine that Alma, at least, went to visit Cassie, not in the hospital but at home, before they left.

Not to me, but around, people told all kinds of stories. I heard them eventually. They said that Rudy Molinaro had been her boyfriend, and that they'd shacked up at the asylum together for days; that Bev had hustled Cassie out of town to keep her from Rudy's clutches. They said that Cassie had threatened to leave for good unless Bev dumped Anders Shute. They said that Anders Shute had been abusing Cassie and her mother only found out when she ran away. They said that Cassie's dad wasn't dead after all, and had invited Cassie — no, Cassie and Bev? — to come and live with him. They said that Cassie's dad wasn't dead; in fact, Cassie's dad was Rudy Molinaro, and she'd been ready to leave her mom for him — no, that they were having an affair and then they only later realized it was incest, that they were father and daughter. They said that she'd tried to kill herself because she was flunking out of school, because she had a drug problem, no, because she'd been gang-raped by a posse of seniors from the lacrosse team. They said that she'd apparently dyed her hair — no, shaven her head? — while on the run. They said she'd had a psychotic break and didn't know where she was when they found her at the asylum. They said that she and I were secret lovers; they said I was jealous of her relationship with Anders/Rudy/Peter and had lured her to the asylum to try to kill her, but had felt remorse just in time. They said that what had really happened was a mystery and none of us would ever know.

I said nothing at all — not even to Jodie — and neither did Peter. I thought it was the one gift of friendship I could properly, if belatedly, give Cassie: to keep to myself the story that I knew, or thought I knew. Let them say what they wanted.

The town, for a while, speculated, analyzed, calculated, imagined. Everybody wanted a story, a story with an arc, with motives and a climax and a resolution. The story that they wanted — no matter what shape they gave it — made Cassie into some sort of victim: a victim of addiction, or abuse, or of her mother's, or of Anders's, or of Rudy's, or even of mine. A corpse would have made the best story, the headliner, and we could all have been devastated, and shocked, and remorseful, and — too late — loving.

Then, only then, relieved of her carnal, sinning self, could Cassie have been immortalized, apotheosized, duly cleansed and elevated. If she'd been murdered, we'd remember her as sweet Cassie, injured Cassie, neglected Cassie, beautiful Cassie, of the azure eyes and fire-white hair, a Cassie purged by suffering. The town of Royston would have claimed and redeemed her.

But because she hadn't '*met her fate*,' as the saying goes, nobody knew what to do with her, with the idea of her — 'a troubled girl,' Mildred Bell murmured sorrowfully behind her counter, the best of them — and after a few baffled, rousing weeks of nonsense, they simply turned away.

At school, mostly within days, people moved on to other things: Sierra Franto's three broken ribs from falling out of the tree outside her bedroom window; Alex Paul's dad, the undertaker, getting in trouble for mixing up two dead grannies at the funeral home. Mostly it was like Instagram: we'd scrolled on; Cassie was just gone from the screen.

⋆ ⋆ ⋆

Before they left, Cassie categorically refused to see me. I emailed and texted her but she didn't reply. I was too wary to call her house, for all sorts of reasons, so finally, in the middle of May, after Cassie had been home from the hospital for a couple of weeks, my mother did. Bev picked up the phone.

'It's so nice of you to call,' she told my mother — in a formal voice, my mother said, as though the two women barely knew each other. 'And we are so incredibly grateful to Julia for her help in finding Cassie.' ('You would have thought,' my father observed, 'that the woman could have picked up the phone herself to call and thank you, wouldn't you? For saving her daughter's life? Just a little thing, after all.') And then Bev went on, 'It's been a tough time, as you can imagine, but especially for Cassie, who has been quite distressed.' My mother noticed this word and repeated it to me, because she was expecting the word 'depressed,' which seemed obvious; but got instead 'distressed,' which, while also true, didn't seem somehow strong enough for the circumstances. 'So,' Bev continued, 'We're trying to look forward, to the future — '

'Of course,' my mother said she said, trying to reassure.

'And that means, in some important ways, closing the door on the past.'

'Of course,' my mother said she said again, although somewhat more uncertainly.

'We're moving away from Royston,' Bev said. 'A fresh start is important.'

'Of course. But when?'

'At the end of next week.'

'My goodness.' My mother couldn't hide her surprise. 'But how will that work? Your whole lives — '

'I've informed the hospice. They understand, these are special circumstances. We can't stay in Royston now.'

My mother was surprised by this too: she wanted to ask *Why not?*, but Bev's manner was so strained, so strange, that she didn't dare. 'Where are you moving to?' she asked instead, as polite as can be.

'I'd rather not say. Don't worry, the good thing about my profession is that there's always work available for someone with my skills.' ('Her profession is death,' my father observed. 'She's not wrong there.')

'But what about Anders?' my mother enquired. 'Surely for a doctor at his level, it takes some time — '

Bev interrupted with a click of the tongue. My mother said she could see in her mind's eye the disapproval on Bev's face, the narrowing of her nostrils and the flattening of her lips. A look with which we were all familiar. 'Anders Shute will not be moving with us,' Bev said. Plain and simple, that sentence only.

'Just you and Cassie?'

'Correct.'

'Oh dear. I see. If it's all so quick — I know how busy you must be — but it would mean so much to Julia, to see Cassie,' my mother said. 'Before you leave — to be able to reassure herself that Cassie really is okay. Because, you know, it was quite traumatic for Julia, the last time she saw Cassie — '

But already, my mother said afterward, she knew from her own entreating tone that she did not expect Bev to say yes.

'That's the thing,' Bev said. 'My Cassie's had a very traumatic time, and anything that might bring it back is, well . . . I'm sorry, but I have to say no. I know you'll understand.'

'Of course,' my mother said again, although she said to me that she didn't understand for a second. 'What about *your* trauma?' my mother said to me. 'It's miraculous that you found her. And dreadful that you had to see her in that state.' She shook her head.

I could tell when we had this conversation — in the kitchen, making dinner, like so many of our conversations, me washing lettuce at the sink, she browning cubed beef for a stew — that my mother was shaken. You could see it in the mad energy with which she poked at the meat.

'I can't fathom it,' she said. 'None of it makes any sense to me.'

My mother didn't know, then, everything that had happened, or at least that Cassie had told Peter had happened, in Bangor, and afterward. I tore at the lettuce leaves as I dropped them into the spinner, turning my back to her. I didn't know whether it would be a betrayal to tell her what I knew. 'What doesn't make sense?' I asked instead.

'It makes you wonder,' she said. 'What you don't know. What's happening all around you, that you can't see.'

We were both quiet a minute, at our tasks.

'I ask myself, Julia, my precious daughter, do I not have any idea what your life is like? Or who you are?'

'Don't be silly, Mom.' But she wasn't entirely wrong. I too was newly aware of the aloneness of each of us, of how little of our selves and lives was shared, even as we shared rooms and hours and conversation. I had known Cassie all my life, knew her gestures and expressions and the timbre of her voice, knew the way her mind worked and her sense of humor and the ways we were alike and the ways we were not. Weren't we secret sisters, umbilically linked? But I had taken my attention from her, and so quickly, it seemed in retrospect, she had changed, things had changed. Days had unfolded, one after the other, months in which I had remained, or considered that I had remained, the same Julia — although who knew, really? — and in those days, while I moved in familiar paths, Cassie's life had altered beyond recognition, behind a scrim, behind the doors of the little house in the cul-de-sac, until what I thought I knew I did not know, and the person I thought I recognized, grew, behind her skin, alien to me. I was oblivious Goya at the Spanish court, and she the French Revolution.

I hadn't known what she was thinking, what she experienced; but still, atavistically, I had known how to find her — she was not so changed as that. What I hadn't anticipated was that she did not want to be found. That the last look she would give me was full of rage.

In the kitchen with my mother, she at the stove and I at the sink, I had for the first time the adult apprehension that my mother too was afraid of this abyss, not as it related to Cassie but as it related to me, to my mother and me. I understood that she had thought to have known me — flesh of her flesh, brought into the world from between her thighs, always beside her, and still, somewhere, inside her — and that she feared, now, maybe for the first time, that she didn't know me at all. I turned and took her in my arms — she was no longer bigger than I was; in fact, I was the taller of us two — and embraced her, and kissed her soft cheek, and whispered in her ear, again, 'Don't be silly,

Mom.' And then, 'There's nothing to be afraid of.' So many times my mother had said these words to me, had made this gesture of love and reassurance; but this was the first time I did it for her. And the first time too that I understood these words might not be true.

* * *

Peter saw Cassie one more time. Not on purpose, and not really to speak to, but he saw her. A couple of days after Bev had shunned my mother, Peter was with his father at Target at nine o'clock at night, after his track meet, picking up dog food, bulk paper towels, and a new charger for his phone. They ran into Cassie and Bev in the wide aisle between makeup and home goods. Pale as milk, Cassie pushed the cart, he said, dwarfed by its red plastic lattice, and her mother practically interposed her body — the voluminous, swishing, scented body — when he approached. They had a pile of white bath towels in the cart, he said, and a gold can of hairspray. He noticed this. Cassie said hi, but she didn't move out from behind the cart, and her eyes, he said, were dull. He thought she was probably on medication, sparrow thin, drifty in her movements. Bev, who had never liked Peter, smiled hard and bright.

'Some last-minute errands,' she brayed. 'So much to do before we go!' And then she pushed Cassie and the cart forcefully into the pet-food aisle — like a kidnapper, Peter said — and that was that. Cassie wore bedroom slippers, the fluffy sheepskin kind. He was hurt that she didn't look back.

'Like she was a hostage,' he said again. 'Like she wasn't herself.'

Whatever that meant.

* * *

For almost a year, Anders Shute didn't go anywhere. He stayed in the little house in the cul-de-sac — he rented it from Bev, I guess, until she sold it the following spring — and when, rarely, you saw him at Bell's or the Rite Aid, he would stretch his thin lips into a smile and incline his head slightly by way of greeting, and move on.

The community broadly surmised, from his presence, that he hadn't done anything wrong, that whatever had transpired in the little house could be summarized simply as 'things didn't work out' or 'Bev and Cassie needed a new start.' But wasn't Anders Shute the source of all of Cassie's despair? Hadn't he destroyed her as surely as Leo the pit bull had savaged her hand? We didn't say this to our parents, and if they had any such thoughts, they didn't express them within our hearing.

Maybe too Anders was an innocent — ill favored, strange and cold, but no more than these unfortunate things. Maybe, Peter and I wondered, it was all about Bev, angel of death. What was true and what wasn't, in Cassie's history? Had her father even been named Burnes? Where had Bev come from, and now where had they gone? Wherever they'd moved to, in such haste, it wasn't because they had 'people' there — as far as we knew, as far as Cassie knew, Bev had no people. And for that matter, maybe wherever they'd gone, they weren't Bev and Cassie Burnes any longer. For months afterward, I'd Google their names and nothing would come up, nothing at all about a life after Royston, as if they'd simply ceased to exist. I hoped that Cassie might write to me, or call, or text, but she never did.

⋆ ⋆ ⋆

By midsummer, Royston had stopped talking about her altogether. Once school was out, kids took up lifeguard and camp-counselor jobs, went on bike trips or to summer school, turned their attention to Jodie's mother's breast-cancer diagnosis, the factory fire at Henkel. The grown-ups had nothing more to say, and so said no more, and then the silence around Cassie grew quieter than the grave, as if Cassie had never existed at all.

Peter and I talked about her a lot, at first, as we held hands and finally as he came to see our friendship as love, the way I'd seen it all along. But we spoke of her less with each passing week. Even between us, who knew as much as anyone knew, we could say only so much before we turned in circles.

Peter was convinced that Bev Burnes had changed their names, that Cassie, wherever she'd gone, was no longer Cassie Burnes. He believed, upon reflection, that Bev was a lifelong fantasist, a con artist, spinning one story after another; and her decade in Royston just one episode in a series of dramas. In his version, there'd never been a Clarke Burnes, and Cassie's football coach in Bangor was pure, strange coincidence. 'Imagine that poor guy,' Peter said, 'with this crazed kid in a beanie on his doorstep, one Monday at dawn, out of the blue. What does that feel like?' I wondered whether Arthur C. Burnes had spoken to his wife, Anna Maria, about it, whether they'd talked about Cassie, whether she was still alive to them somehow.

Peter thought that Bev had had a different name to begin with — did we even know where she was supposed to have grown up? Rochester, New York? Lancaster, Pennsylvania? Outside Wilmington? Why did nobody know for sure, and why had nobody noticed that they didn't know? Peter thought that Bev was like one of those grifters on crime television, a made-up name, a false identity, out delivering death across the country with her bag of morphine and oxycodone and fentanyl — the angel of mercy, so-called. Maybe, he said, Bev never even knew who Cassie's father was. Potentially, Cassie wasn't even Bev's child.

'You're going too far,' I said; and he said, 'Why? It happens.'

I didn't want to believe that the solid history of my childhood could unravel altogether, simply at our whim. 'It doesn't happen very often,' I replied. 'We know these people.' I was ready to blame Anders Shute: his appearance in their lives, his seduction of Bev; his sinister interest in controlling Cassie, which might have evolved in any number of ways. She'd never confided anything specific either to Peter or to me, but something had been wrong in that house. We both knew that. Why not believe, as Cassie had believed, in the reality of Clarke Burnes? Why not believe for Cassie, as Cassie had believed for her vanished cat, Electra, that she was living another, better life somewhere nearby, eating her meals off silver plates and destined for a beautiful future?

I want fiercely to believe it, for myself as much as for her. All our stories are more or less made up, after all. What doesn't seem imaginary — what feels most real — is my nightmare about Cassie and the poisoned cloak, my sense that this is what it means to grow up. Whatever choices we think we make, whatever we think we can control, has a life and a destiny we cannot fully see. That I can sense the way the plot will go, that I could, on that Saturday morning in April a couple of years ago, save the life of one Cassie Burnes — it's only an illusion I cling to. What will be will be, irrespective, not because fate is unassailable but because none of us ever sees face-to-face: through a glass darkly is the best we can manage.

* * *

Last night at supper, my parents started up the college conversation again. This coming fall it will be time for me to apply. We sat perspiring around the kitchen table with the windows open to the slight breeze and the sunset casting shafts of light and shadow across the garden, the maples in silhouette against the bloody western sky. We could hear tree frogs and the distant sounds of the Saghafi kids in their pool ('Marco . . . ' ' . . . Polo'). My father raised the subject: we need to plan some college visits for August, before school starts.

He tipped back in his chair — which annoys my mother, who thinks each time that he will fall and who resents the scuff marks on the floor — and spoke without looking at me, as much as to say my reply was a matter of complete indifference to him. 'Any thoughts?'

'I want to act,' I said, which wasn't new, of course, but new for me to put this ambition first.

'Of course you do, sweetie.' My mother sliced seconds of quiche unasked and slipped them onto our plates. 'But that's not how you choose a college.'

'Why not?'

'Sure, Carole, why not?' My father banged down on all four chair legs and wielded his fork. 'If she wants to act, what's wrong with that?'

'You don't get a *degree* in acting,' my mother said.

'Maybe not,' I said, 'but I can choose what places interest me based on whether they've got good theatre programs.'

'What's so appealing about acting?' my mother asked. She wants me to be interested in politics, or science; she sees it as a woman's obligation, even now. To her, acting is passive, secondhand

— you're saying lines that somebody else wrote, and pretending to be somebody you're not.

'Come off it, Carole, give the girl a break.'

'I'm not hassling, I'm genuinely curious.'

'Do I really have to explain?'

'Give it a try,' my mother said. She had on her interested-grown-up expression, her eyebrows raised, a slight, forced smile on her lips.

'You can't say it's culturally irrelevant.' I was aware that I sounded defensive. 'There's nothing our culture cares about more.'

'Than the *theatre?*'

'Than acting. Okay, TV, movies, whatever. It's what we Americans *do*.'

'You've lost me there,' my dad smiled. 'I'm an American, and I'm a dentist. I care about teeth.'

'You know what I mean.'

'No, really, dear. Explain it to us.'

'I just like to act, okay? Won't that do?'

My father patted the back of my hand on the table. 'Of course it will,' he said. 'Your mom's being a bully. We know you love it, and that's fine.' He paused. 'She just wants you to think about why. Because maybe there'd be other things, I don't know, alternatives, that might be as interesting for you to consider. Not instead, you know, but in addition.'

'Like curing cancer, you mean?'

He laughed. 'Kind of like that.'

I shook my head. We changed the subject.

How could I have explained that it all seems like acting, like theatre, to me? Each of us puts on our costumes, our masks, and pretends. We take the vast, inchoate, ungraspable swell of events and emotions that surrounds us and in which we are immersed, and we funnel it into a simplified narrative, a simple story that we represent as true. Like: I love avocadoes but detest Brussels sprouts. Or: I'm great at English but no good at math. Or: I'm a loyal friend who'll do anything for the people I love. Or: I know you so well I can anticipate your every move. Or: I know myself, and this is what it's like to be me.

But we don't really know anything at all, except how the story should go, and we make believe it's our story, hoping everything will turn out okay. The difference is that onstage, or in a film, we acknowledge the artifice, we accept that we've made a world that excludes what we ignore. Like gods, we invent a world that makes sense.

* * *

In the film of Cassie's life, she recovers from her grief (because everything she went through can be summarized as grief), and Bev is restored to her as Cassie once and for a long time believed Bev to be — the plump, geeky, intensely loving mother who is her staunch ally in a lonely world. In the film, Cassie begins again, in a high school in Stamford, Connecticut, or in Atlanta, Georgia, or in Portland, Oregon, a new chapter, in which she can be anyone she wants to be, popular and successful and undamaged and free, heading to her immaculate future.

In this new life, where the darkness of the

Bonnybrook is forever forgotten, she swims, glides perfectly through long golden afternoons in crystalline water, like the water at the quarry. The bottom is never murky, or treacherous, and she knows she will never drown. And when we see that film — if they ever make it, if it's ever released — we'll say: Yes, of course. *This* is what it means to be a young woman; this is the true story, this beautiful vision: Cassie's calm strokes and their gentle ripples; her ribboning white-blond hair; the smooth, dappled green water overhung, along the shore, with branches; the boulders of tawny stone; immense, above, the blue, blue sky. *This* is what we will never forget.

Acknowledgments

My heartfelt gratitude to my wise and generous editor, Jill Bialosky, and to the amazing team at W. W. Norton; and also to Ursula Doyle, Charlie King, and everyone at Fleet/Little, Brown UK. Infinite thanks to Sarah Chalfant and Andrew Wylie, my agents, extraordinary champions and stellar human beings.

My loving thanks, too, to dear family and friends for support through thick and thin: to James, my love and first reader; to Lucian, for keeping us laughing; and to Livia, my second reader, whose perspective and suggestions were invaluable.

Thanks also to Louise Glück for her poem 'Midsummer,' an inspiration.

We do hope that you have enjoyed reading this large print book.

Did you know that all of our titles are available for purchase?

We publish a wide range of high quality large print books including:

Romances, Mysteries, Classics
General Fiction
Non Fiction and Westerns

Special interest titles available in large print are:

The Little Oxford Dictionary
Music Book
Song Book
Hymn Book
Service Book

Also available from us courtesy of Oxford University Press:

Young Readers' Dictionary
(large print edition)
Young Readers' Thesaurus
(large print edition)

For further information or a free brochure, please contact us at:

Ulverscroft Large Print Books Ltd.,
The Green, Bradgate Road, Anstey,
Leicester, LE7 7FU, England.
Tel: (00 44) **0116 236 4325**
Fax: (00 44) **0116 234 0205**

Other titles published by Ulverscroft:

A BORDER STATION

Shane Connaughton

For the son of the local sergeant in an isolated Garda station on the border between Cavan and Fermanagh, life is balanced between the brooding, taciturn presence of his father, whom he loves and fears in equal measure, and the reassurance of his warm and witty mother. His world is narrowed to lakes, woods, hayfields, country lanes and the amazing characters he encounters — tinkers, drinkers, publicans, policemen, farmers and the tantalising older sister of his Protestant friend. Amidst the drumlins and bogs, the boy's imagination roams free and unfettered. And at night, lulled by the rhythm of his mother's fleecy breathing, he finds solace. But change is coming. It's time to grow up . . .

THE WOMAN ON THE ORIENT EXPRESS

Lindsay Jayne Ashford

Hoping to make a clean break from a fractured marriage, Agatha Christie boards the Orient Express in disguise. But unlike her famous detective Hercule Poirot, she can't neatly unravel the mysteries she encounters on this fateful journey. And Agatha isn't the only passenger on board with secrets. Her cabinmate Katharine Keeling's first marriage ended in tragedy, propelling her toward a second relationship mired in deceit. Nancy Nelson, newly married but carrying another man's child, is desperate to conceal the pregnancy and teeters on the brink of utter despair. Each woman hides her past from the others, ferociously guarding her secrets. But as the train bound for the Middle East speeds down the track, the parallel courses of their lives shift to intersect — with lasting repercussions.

THIS WAS A MAN

Jeffrey Archer

The conclusion to the Clifton Chronicles. Giles Barrington discovers the truth about his wife Karin from the cabinet secretary. Is she a spy, or a pawn in a larger game? Harry Clifton sets out to write his magnum opus, while his wife Emma completes her ten years as chairman of the Bristol Royal Infirmary, and receives an unexpected call from Margaret Thatcher offering her a job. Sebastian Clifton becomes chairman of Farthings Kaufman bank after Hakim Bishara resigns for personal reasons. Sebastian and his wife Samantha's talented daughter Jessica is expelled from the Slade School of Art. Lady Virginia is about to flee the country to avoid her creditors when the Duchess of Hertford dies, and she sees an opportunity to finally trump the Cliftons and the Barringtons. Then tragedy engulfs the Clifton family . . .

WILDEST OF ALL

P. K. Lynch

The Donnelly family are a tight-knit bunch. But when one of their own dies without warning, the mother, daughter-in-law and daughter, despite being united in grief, are each sent hurtling in wildly different directions. From the churches of Glasgow to the nightclubs of London, can they find their way back to each other before it's too late? And in the wake of a parent's death, who exactly is responsible for looking after whom?